"Tell them to send more help," McCoy instructed the pilot.

The three members of Disaster Relief pushed the crowd of survivors back to make room for the take-off. They had barely cleared a path when the *Mead* zoomed off into the azure skies. Within seconds it was gone, and there was a frightened murmur in the crowd. It was as if all their hope had gone with the shuttlecraft.

DISCARD

Lisa let out a sigh. "It's just us now, and there are so many of them to help."

"The transporters are working at the moment," said McCoy. "We transported twenty-two criticals out."

Spock nodded with approval. "We have fulfilled our first two objectives—we delivered supplies and evacuated the injured. We should try to find individuals who are trapped and need immediate help."

McCoy nodded. "Okay, let's ask around."

Suddenly there came a low roar from the depths of Playamar, and the ground beneath McCoy's feet began to pitch and roll. It bucked like a trampoline, and McCoy staggered toward the gaping chasm. . . .

Star Trek: The Next Generation
STARFLEET ACADEMY

Star Trek:
STARFLEET ACADEMY

Star Trek: Deep Space Nine

Star Trek movie tie-in

Star Trek Generations

Available from MINSTREL Books

STAR TREK®
STARFLEET ACADEMY

#2: AFTERSHOCK

JOHN VORNHOLT

Interior illustrations by
Todd Cameron Hamilton

A MINSTREL® BOOK

Published by POCKET BOOKS
New York   London   Toronto   Sydney   Tokyo   Singapore

A MINSTREL PAPERBACK *Original*

A Minstrel Book published by
POCKET BOOKS, a division of Simon & Schuster Inc.
1230 Avenue of the Americas, New York, NY 10020

This book is published by Pocket Books, a division of Simon & Schuster Inc., under exclusive license from Paramount Pictures.

ISBN: 0-671-00079-9

First Minstrel Books printing September 1996

10 9 8 7 6 5 4 3 2 1

A MINSTREL BOOK and colophon are registered trademarks of Simon & Schuster Inc.

Cover art by Michael Herring

Printed in the U.S.A.

For Hayley, Anna, and Piper

STARFLEET TIMELINE

1969 Neil Armstrong walks on Earth's moon.

2156 Romulan Wars begin between Earth forces and the Romulan Star Empire.

2160 Romulan peace treaty signed, establishing the Neutral Zone.

2161 United Federation of Planets formed; Starfleet established with charter "to boldly go where no man has gone before."

2218 First contact with the Klingon Empire.

2245 Starship *U.S.S. Enterprise* NCC-1701 launched on its first five-year mission under the command of Captain Robert April and First Officer Christopher Pike.

2249 Spock enters Starfleet Academy as the first Vulcan student. Leonard McCoy enters Starfleet Medical School.

2250 James T. Kirk enters Starfleet Academy.

2251 Christopher Pike assumes command of the *Enterprise* for its second five-year mission.

Starfleet Timeline

2252   Spock, still a Starfleet cadet, begins serving under Captain Pike on the *Enterprise*.

2253   Spock graduates from Starfleet Academy. Leonard McCoy graduates from Starfleet Medical School.

2254   James T. Kirk graduates from Starfleet Academy. As a lieutenant, Kirk is assigned duty aboard the *U.S.S. Farragut*.

2261   *U.S.S. Enterprise*, under the command of Captain Christopher Pike, completes its third five-year mission.

2263   James T. Kirk is promoted to captain of the *Enterprise* and meets Christopher Pike, who is promoted to fleet captain.

2264   Captain James T. Kirk, in command of the *U.S.S. Enterprise*, embarks on a historic five-year mission of exploration.

2266   Dr. Leonard McCoy replaces Dr. Mark Piper as chief medical officer aboard the *Enterprise*.

2269   Kirk's original five-year mission ends, and Starship *Enterprise* returns to spacedock. Kirk is promoted to admiral.

Starfleet Timeline

2271   *U.S.S. Enterprise* embarks on Kirk's second five-year mission (*Star Trek: The Motion Picture*).

2277   James T. Kirk accepts a teaching position at Starfleet Academy; Spock assumes command of the Starship *Enterprise*.

2285   In orbit around the Genesis planet, Kirk orders the destruction of the Starship *Enterprise* to prevent the ship from falling into Klingon hands (*Star Trek III: The Search for Spock*).

2286   Kirk is demoted to captain and assigned command of the Starship *Enterprise* NCC-1701-A (*Star Trek IV: The Voyage Home*).

2287   The *Enterprise* is commandeered by Sybok, Spock's half-brother, and taken to the center of the galaxy (*Star Trek V: The Final Frontier*).

2292   Alliance between the Klingon Empire and the Romulan Star Empire collapses.

2293   The Klingon Empire launches a major peace initiative; the crews of the *U.S.S. Enterprise* and the *U.S.S. Excelsior*, captained by Hikaru Sulu, thwart a conspiracy to sabotage the Khitomer Peace Conference. Afterward, the *Enterprise-A* is decommissioned, and Kirk retires from Starfleet.

U.S.S. Enterprise NCC-1701-B, under the command of Captain John Harriman, is severely damaged on her maiden voyage. Honored guest Captain James T. Kirk is listed as missing, presumed killed in action.

2344 *U.S.S. Enterprise* NCC-1701-C, under the command of Captain Rachel Garrett, is destroyed while defending the Klingon outpost on Narendra III from Romulan attack.

2346 Romulan massacre of Klingon outpost on Khitomer.

2364 Captain Jean-Luc Picard assumes command of the *U.S.S. Enterprise* NCC-1701-D.

2367 Borg attack at Wolf 359; *U.S.S. Saratoga* destroyed; First Officer Lieutenant Commander Benjamin Sisko and his son, Jake, are among the survivors; *Enterprise* defeats the Borg vessel in orbit around Earth.

2369 Commander Benjamin Sisko assumes command of Deep Space Nine in orbit over Bajor.

Starfleet Timeline

2371   *U.S.S. Enterprise* NCC-1701-D destroyed on Veridian III.

Former *Enterprise* captain James T. Kirk emerges from a temporal nexus, but dies helping Picard save the Veridian system.

U.S.S. Voyager, under the command of Captain Kathryn Janeway, is accidentally transported to the Delta Quadrant. The crew begins a 70-year journey back to Federation space.

2372   The Klingon Empire's attempted invasion of Cardassia Prime results in the dissolution of the Khitomer peace treaty between the Federation and the Klingon Empire.

Source: *Star Trek® Chronology* / Michael Okuda and Denise Okuda

Chapter
1

Leonard H. McCoy heaved a sigh and sunk his bony frame into a plush armchair. It was too plush, because too many Starfleet cadets had sunk into it over the years. A spring stuck him in the rump, which only added to his grumpiness.

He bolted to his feet and set his electronic clipboard on the table. McCoy looked a bit odd standing there in his gray cadet jumpsuit with a white bathrobe over his shoulders, but he always found the dormitory lounge to be cold. *Heck, all of San Francisco is cold to this Southern boy.*

It was late, his roommate was snoring, and McCoy had to study for an exam in metabolic stasis procedures. Weird instruments, keeping people alive indefinitely—it wasn't his favorite kind of medicine, and he was worried about tomorrow's test.

McCoy wasn't a doctor yet, just a medical student. He was a transfer student, too, so he was a little older than most of the new cadets at Starfleet Academy. He did fine in his studies, but he still didn't feel part of the academy lifestyle.

So many of the younger cadets wanted to be explorers and starship captains. They knew exactly what they wanted, but McCoy just wanted to survive day by day. Cadets were dropping out of the academy med school every day, because it was tougher than regular schools. He must've been crazy to come here.

Also McCoy hated to admit that he was homesick. He was from a little town in Georgia, and he hadn't been home in several years. But he was going home over the winter break. Just one more week to go!

McCoy could see the old Civil War monument in the town square, the Spanish moss hanging from the oaks, and the red clay banks of the lake. His dad would be catching lots of fat catfish and bluegills by now. He wanted to be there, helping him catch, clean, and eat those whoppers.

It was hard to imagine that he would get two whole weeks off from his crushing schedule. Thoughts of fried catfish and long naps on the porch kept him going through this last terrible week of exams.

McCoy's homesick daydream was interrupted by Hibulta, a big, hairless Delosian. He rushed through the lobby and pointed at the cadet. "Good, you're still up."

"Why is that good?" grumbled McCoy. "I'd rather be asleep."

"Stay awake, McCoy." The Delosian charged off.

2

McCoy just shook his head. Everybody at the academy called everybody by their last name. So he was beginning to think of himself as "McCoy" instead of "Leonard." It was just one more adjustment he had to make to life at the academy.

He had finally settled into a safe spot on the sofa and was picking up his clipboard, when a squad of cadets burst into the lounge. Hibulta was in the lead, along with Wainwright, a big blond cadet.

"Okay, McCoy," said Hibulta, "you're with us!"

"I'm with *you?*" drawled McCoy. "What on earth are you talking about?"

Wainwright stepped forward. "Come on, McCoy, the freshmen dorm has challenged us to a game of touch football. Our honor is on the line."

McCoy sat up at the mention of football, a fine, old Southern tradition. It wasn't an official sport at Starfleet Academy, but it hung around, refusing to die. Sometimes he played football with the guys, when he was trying to fit in, but tonight he had too much studying to do.

"You boys go ahead," said McCoy. "I plan to go to bed tonight without any broken bones."

"It's just *touch* football," said Hibulta. "And we've only got ten guys—we're one short."

"And we know you can catch the ball," added Wainwright. "You can't do much else, but you can do that."

McCoy scoffed at the offhand compliment. "You make it sound like lots of fun, but I've got to study."

"Better we play with ten guys than with him," said another cadet. "He's just a coward."

3

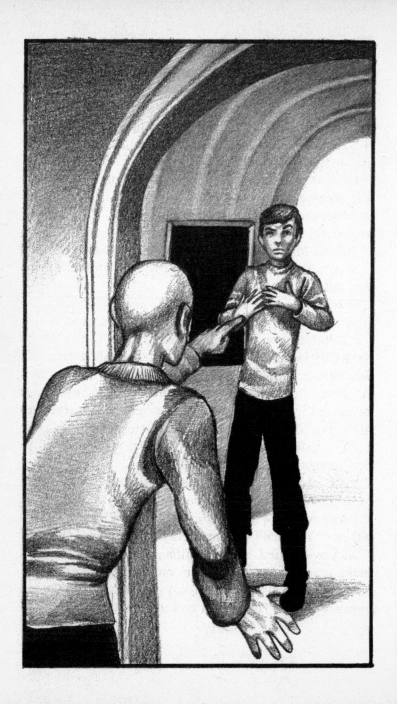

Now McCoy bolted upright in his seat. "Somebody is going to have to take back that last remark."

There was a chorus of shouts. "Come on and play!" "McCoy, we need you!"

"All right," grumbled McCoy as he dragged himself to his feet. He supposed he should be flattered that they asked him to play. Of course, there was nobody else awake at two o'clock in the morning.

He followed his ragtag teammates out the door, down a sidewalk, to the campus green. The green was a big field at the center of the academy, a pleasant place to pass a few moments on the way from one class to another. It had a well-lit, well-manicured lawn, perfect for touch football.

McCoy shivered in the cool ocean breeze, wishing he was still wearing his bathrobe. Under the moonlight and the flood lamps, he could see the other team starting to gather. Just a bunch of pathetic, first-year cadets, he told himself. Nothing to worry about.

They weren't really supposed to be doing this, of course. At two o'clock in the morning, who was going to find out? In one way, he decided, it was good for them to cast off some of the tension that came with final exams. The campus green had seen plenty of impromptu football games over the years.

"Okay, the babies are here," said Wainwright, referring to the underclassmen. McCoy sometimes saw women in these games, but not tonight. They had better sense, he guessed.

A cocky freshman bounced out of the crowd and

pointed at the upperclassmen. "Are we here to play or talk?"

"Play! Play!" came the cry from both sides.

That was when McCoy noticed that the team of freshmen had many more than eleven players, while his team had only eleven. They could substitute players, and his team couldn't. That was McCoy's first hint that they were going to have trouble with these upstarts.

They flipped a coin, and his team lost. Eleven players from each side took the field. McCoy watched Hibulta line up the ball, step back, and kick off. The game was under way!

McCoy whirled around to see two freshmen steaming toward him. Both of them were trying to block him, and he didn't even have a chance to duck. They fell on top of him, burying him in the thick grass. Touch football meant no tackling, but it didn't mean no blocking.

Luckily, his teammates tagged the runner before he got very far. McCoy stood up and looked angrily at his grass-stained jumpsuit. Now they had made him mad!

McCoy chose to play pass defense. He would let somebody else smash into the big guys at the line. The first-year cadets tried to run on their first play, and Hibulta tagged the runner at the goal line. The upper-class team hooted in victory, but that was only one play.

It's hard to run in touch football, thought McCoy. *This time they'll try a pass.*

"The wideout!" McCoy shouted as the younger cadets broke from their huddle.

"You take him!" yelled Wainwright.

McCoy looked at the muscular cadet across from him.

It was one of those who had blocked him on the kickoff. The sandy-haired cadet looked like a born athlete, and McCoy wasn't sure he could win a footrace with him. But he was sure the pass was going to go right at him.

The ball was hiked, and the young cadet streaked down the side of the lawn. McCoy tried to stay ahead of him, but it was a losing proposition. Just as the ball was thrown, McCoy stuck out his leg and tripped the freshman. The ball sailed harmlessly over their heads.

"Hey, you tripped me!" complained the cadet as he jumped to his feet.

McCoy shrugged. "It's hard to play out here in the moonlight. Sometimes your feet get tangled up."

"Yeah, right," grumbled the kid.

The next play, they tried a sweep around the side, away from McCoy. The runner had good blocking, and he made twenty meters before Wainwright pushed him off his feet. That was the trouble with touch football— the "touch" could get a little hard.

The next play was going to be another pass, McCoy could feel it. He saw the sandy-haired cadet he had tripped—he was lining up in the backfield. McCoy would have to cover somebody else, but he was sure that the ball was going to the cocky young cadet.

When the ball was snapped, McCoy ignored the man he was supposed to cover and raced across the field to try to break up the pass. He was too late, as the muscular cadet raced by the defender and caught the ball in stride.

McCoy had good position, but the kid danced left and right, trying to fake him out. McCoy finally threw himself at the kid's feet, and he trampled him and just kept running.

"Hey, I touched you!" groaned McCoy from the ground.

The young man ran back and grinned at him. "Yeah, you were lucky."

"Come on, let's stop them!" yelled Wainwright. "Hey, McCoy, get there faster next time!"

"He wasn't even my man," grumbled McCoy as he picked himself up.

The underclass dorm put in almost a whole new team for the next series of plays. Three plays later, they scored a touchdown on the panting upperclassman.

Uh-oh, thought McCoy, *this could be a long night.*

But at least they were going to get the ball, finally. The freshman kicked off, and the ball sailed over McCoy's head to the man behind him. He looked around for somebody to block, and there was that same cocky freshman. McCoy tried to block him but he never laid a finger on the kid.

The upperclass dorm finally got a chance to score. In the huddle, Wainwright looked directly at McCoy. "Line up right and go long. Milkins, you go short across the middle. Lechemor, you go to the flats and wait. You're the dump-off man. Everyone else block."

McCoy was not surprised when he lined up and saw the same muscular, sandy-haired cadet lining up across from him. *Well, it was time to show this kid a thing or two.*

Wainwright grunted a few times, and the center hiked the ball. McCoy started toward the middle, then broke toward the outside. He hoped that would fake out the kid, but he was right with him, step for step. Wainwright had to throw it to the short man, who only made a few yards.

The young cadet was smiling at McCoy. "Doesn't look like they want to throw it to you."

"Probably not," agreed McCoy. "You can take it easy."

When he got back to the huddle, he told the quarterback, "My guy is sort of short. Let me come back for it, and throw it to me high."

"Right," agreed Wainwright. "Same play. Let's block this time."

They lined up again, and McCoy tried not to even look at the young cadet who was dogging him. At the snap, he ran straight down the middle, and the defender was running right with him. Then McCoy stopped short and took a few steps back.

Wainwright was looking at him, and he cut loose with the ball—high as expected. The unlucky freshman had to skid to a stop and double back. He didn't have much energy to jump, and McCoy plucked the ball off his fingertips and cradled it to his chest.

He was running down the field, thinking it was TD time, when he heard what sounded like a bull behind him. McCoy peered over his shoulder to see the cocky kid coming hard. In the cool air he was snorting steam, and his arms and legs were churning like an engine.

The freshman was gaining, so McCoy dashed for the sidelines. Only there weren't any sidelines, because this

wasn't a real field—so he ran off the lawn toward a fence. His pursuer kept coming, and he leapt at McCoy.

He thudded into McCoy's midsection, and the two of them crashed through a row of hedges. They rolled up against the fence, with McCoy wheezing and gasping for breath. At once, shrieking sirens started to blare, and the area was bathed in throbbing pink light.

"You idiot!" snapped McCoy.

"I'm sorry," said the kid. "I forgot it was touch, not tackle."

"That was stupid enough, but then you ran us into a security fence!"

"What?"

McCoy threw the football, and it bounced off an invisible forcefield. The freshman stood up and ran his hands along the barrier, which twinkled at his touch.

"We're in trouble," said the young cadet.

"No kidding." With a groan, McCoy sat up and gazed past the broken shrubbery at the lawn. The other players had run for it—he couldn't see any of them. This close to winter break, who wanted to stick around and get into trouble?

He wagged his finger at the young cadet. "If you're going to wash out of the academy, that's fine with me. But next time leave me out of it!"

"Maybe there's a way out of this mess." The freshman gave him a boyish grin.

McCoy could only scowl as red-shirted Security forces surrounded them. He saw one phaser, but most of the officers had tricorders and were scanning the intruders.

"Starfleet Security," said a stern voice. "Identify yourselves."

"Cadet Leonard H. McCoy, medical branch."

"Cadet James T. Kirk, first year."

Chapter
2

The next day went as badly as possible, with McCoy doing poorly on his stasis exam, he was sure. He was barely awake after spending most of the night in the custody of Starfleet Security. Then he had the entire day to dread his appointment with Admiral Ybarra.

The Superintendent of Starfleet Academy had his office inside a clear pyramid on the roof of quadrangle C. Interior walls gave the impression of building blocks that didn't exist, because the outer walls were smooth. McCoy paused as he got off the lift and stared at the imposing structure.

The door of another lift opened behind him, and McCoy turned to see Cadet Kirk stroll jauntily off. The idiot actually smiled at McCoy as if he were glad to see him.

"What are you so happy about?" growled McCoy.

Kirk shrugged. "I've never met Admiral Ybarra before. This is a chance to impress him."

"Impress him?" roared McCoy. "You're here because you crashed into a security fence in the middle of the night. They don't give medals for that."

The cadet smiled confidently and strode toward the gleaming pyramid. The doors opened at his approach, and McCoy hunched his shoulders and followed him in. They came to attention in front of an ensign in the lobby, and she pointed them toward the admiral's inner office.

McCoy glanced upward at the clear ceiling, which softly filtered a gray San Francisco day. He could tell by the slope of the ceiling that they were delving deeper into the pyramid, toward its center. Kirk bravely led the way, marching to his own funeral, thought McCoy.

They both slowed to enter the center of the pyramid, where four translucent walls met at a pinnacle overhead. The ceiling was so high that the office felt like a cathedral. The meticulous admiral had added to the pyramid's design with lots of stark, clear furniture. McCoy would have been afraid to sit on any of it.

Ybarra was a small man of Eurasian descent. He sat at his translucent desk going over some documents with a female captain. He ignored McCoy and Kirk, but she glanced at them with mild curiosity. The admiral and the captain conversed in low tones until they finally agreed.

"At ease," said the admiral. "This is Captain Vrena, and we've been discussing your misconduct."

"Permission to speak, sir," asked Kirk.

The admiral peered at him through sharp black eyes. "If you're going to make some kind of excuse, you can

forget it. That was a sensitive research-and-development site you crashed into. Even if it was accidental, it was still a breach of security, and we take a dim view of breaches of security."

He stared from Kirk to McCoy. "Do I make myself clear?"

"Yes, sir!" they both answered. Kirk snapped his mouth shut.

The admiral folded his hands in front of him. "Seeing as the two of you have so much excess energy, perhaps it would be a good idea if you volunteered for one of our service clubs. Captain Vrena has a few suggestions."

The woman cleared her throat. "Cadet McCoy, the Disaster Relief Service Club is in particular need of medics. You qualify with your premedical training, and we are conducting training classes next week, during the break."

McCoy gasped. "You mean, I wouldn't get to go home during break?"

"Cadet," said Admiral Ybarra, "Starfleet is about duty. The Disaster Relief Service Club is in urgent need of medics. It's a dirty, dangerous job, but you get to save lives. Moreover, I would think that the break wouldn't be enjoyable knowing you have disciplinary action looming over your heads. Am I right?"

"Yes, sir," answered McCoy, snapping to attention. "I volunteer."

The admiral nodded with approval. "There is a membership drive going on now in quadrangle A. Report over there and sign up."

"I'll do Disaster Relief, too," offered Kirk.

Captain Vrena smiled slightly. "No, Cadet Kirk, we have another service club that is also dirty and dangerous. Would you like to try that?"

"Yes, sir!" said Kirk proudly.

"Good." She nodded with approval. "I'll put you down for mess duty. Report to the kitchen."

Kirk gulped. "The kitchen? Mess duty?"

"Yes, and I like my potatoes sliced thin," added Ybarra.

"But, sir, this . . . this *sawbones* gets exciting duty, and I get kitchen duty. It isn't fair."

The admiral stiffened in his chair. "Let me tell you something, mister, there is nothing fair about Starfleet. Today you may get mess duty, and tomorrow you may be the youngest captain in the fleet. You have to take the good with the bad. Dismissed."

McCoy and Kirk hustled out. Heads downcast, they strolled through the pyramid until they were outside on the roof again, both of them glum and deep in thought.

Kirk pounded his fist into his palm. "I'm going to take over that kitchen, and turn it into the best kitchen Starfleet Academy ever had."

"Good for you," said McCoy. "Meanwhile, you ruined my winter break, and I won't get home again for eight months, if then. I needed to spend some time with my dad."

"Homesick, huh?" Kirk nodded sympathetically. "You have to get over that."

"Oh, listen to the voice of experience."

They stopped at the lift that went to ground level. McCoy let Kirk get on, then he stepped back.

"You're not coming with me?" asked the young cadet.

"No," said McCoy, "I never want to see you again. You're nothing but trouble."

"It might be hard to avoid me. See you around, Sawbones." The lift door shut on James T. Kirk and took him out of McCoy's life forever, or so he hoped.

The dejected cadet made his way to quadrangle A, where the recruiting drive for the service clubs was taking place. He still couldn't believe he was going to be stuck in San Francisco over winter break. Not only that, but he had probably done badly on the stasis exam. Maybe Starfleet wasn't the place for him after all.

McCoy tried to concentrate on the words of Admiral Ybarra: "Disaster relief is a dirty, dangerous job, but you get to save lives." Wasn't that the reason he wanted to be a doctor? Then what was he complaining about? Maybe it would be fun. At least it sounded better than kitchen duty.

But he couldn't stop thinking about the lost opportunity to go home. He was frightened by the course he was on, a course that would take him into space, to far-off worlds. Maybe his yearning for home was his heart telling him that he was making a mistake.

Maybe he just wanted to see friendly faces and sleep under his old quilt. The worst of it was that they were expecting him, and he would have to call to tell them he wasn't coming.

McCoy's spirits were still low when he followed several other cadets into the lobby of quadrangle A. Four color-coded elevators surrounded him and branched off toward different dorm towers, but he was looking for the recruiters. He was thinking that he might as well get it over with.

He found directions on the information console, which told new members to go to the recreation room. McCoy went down a flight of stairs and found himself in a game room that had everything from Ping-Pong tables to three-dimensional chess. Card tables and signs were set up for the various service clubs.

He saw the Mechanics Club, which recycled old equipment into useful stuff. There was also the Hospice Club, which visited sick and elderly people. There was another club to work on archaeological digs, one running a food drive, another planting trees, and many more.

Seeing all this goodwill, McCoy wondered why he had never volunteered for a service club before. He knew they existed and that they did good work, plus they looked good on one's record. But he had always been so wrapped up in his own problems that he had never had time to volunteer. Or so he thought.

McCoy was finally feeling good about this sudden turn of events when he spotted the table for Disaster Relief. As he strode closer, he only saw one person at the table—a tall, dark-haired cadet who looked very somber.

Then McCoy spotted the pointed ears and odd skin tone, and he stopped short. Was that a Vulcan? He hadn't talked to any Vulcans before, although he had seen a few of them around campus. Did they really have green blood? He wondered.

McCoy put on a cheerful face as he approached the table. "I'd like to sign up!" He added nervously, "In fact, I *have* to sign up, if you get my drift."

The Vulcan raised an eyebrow, but gave him no other expression. "This is a volunteer club. Would you like me to tell you about it?"

McCoy lowered his voice. "There's no need. The admiral suggested I sign up."

"Are you volunteering or not?" asked the solemn Vulcan.

"No, I didn't volunteer," answered McCoy, getting

angry as he thought about what had happened to him. "It was all the fault of that stupid freshman, Kirk!"

"Then you should not join. This is a volunteer service club, and to join against your will is illogical."

McCoy blinked in amazement. "What kind of cock-eyed, bubble-brained thinking is that?"

"It is called logic."

"Listen, you . . . do you have a name?"

"Yes, I do. Spock."

"Okay, Cadet Spock, does this service club need medics?"

"Yes, we are in dire need of medics."

"Well, I'm a medical student! I already have most of the training, so go ahead and sign me up!"

The Vulcan held up an electronic clipboard. "We have a volunteer form, and only volunteers are allowed to fill it out. You do not appear to be a volunteer."

McCoy was sputtering now. "Listen, you pointy-eared popinjay, what would it take for you to let me join?"

"A full understanding of what you are joining," answered the Vulcan. "Before choosing Disaster Relief, I studied every service club thoroughly. This club makes the most effective use of academy resources and personnel. Even so, we have been understaffed for four-point-three years, resulting in a twelve percent decrease in efficiency from our peak performance."

"Good help is hard to find," McCoy grumbled.

Spock nodded. "Precisely. Certain aspects of this club repel volunteers, such as the rigorous training and the likelihood of being called to a dangerous mission any

time. All volunteers should be aware that there is danger and grueling work involved."

"You make it sound real attractive," said McCoy. "What do I care if the superintendent of the academy likes me or not? I can always be a small-town doctor somewhere."

The Vulcan added, "Last year we saved three hundred twelve lives on five different planets."

"By George!" exclaimed McCoy, "that sounds like a logical thing to do! Okay, I volunteer."

Spock offered him the clipboard and a stylus. "You are aware that the first week of winter break is devoted to training."

McCoy's shoulders slumped. "Yes, I know that. Do you think we can go home for the second week?"

"I presume so, but you should ask Captain Raelius, our faculty advisor."

McCoy nodded and finished filling out the form. "What is the training like?"

"I do not know. I will be taking the training for the first time myself."

"And you're the recruiter?" McCoy shook his head. "No wonder they can't get anybody to sign up."

"I am merely filling in," answered Spock.

"I know what you mean," said McCoy. Just as he was about to walk away, an attractive female cadet strolled up to the table. She had beautiful brown hair, and she smiled pleasantly at both of them.

"My name is Lisa Donald, and I'd like some information on Disaster Relief."

"We have been understaffed for four-point-three

years," said Spock, "resulting in a twelve percent decrease in efficiency from our peak performance evaluation."

McCoy stepped in front of the Vulcan and turned on the Southern charm. "What my friend is trying to say, Lisa, is that we really need you to volunteer. But only if you want to save lives, go to exotic places, and take a few risks. We do all the things you joined Starfleet to do!"

"That sounds great," said Lisa Donald. "What is the training like?"

"Oh, it's fun," claimed McCoy. "It only takes a week, and there's lots of fresh air and exercise!"

Spock nodded thoughtfully. "There will be considerable exercise."

"I'll sign up," said Lisa. Spock handed her the clipboard.

McCoy smiled at the young lady. "A wise choice. Can I buy you a cup of coffee to celebrate?"

"Not right now, thanks. I'm meeting my boyfriend."

"You're meeting with your boyfriend," said McCoy glumly. "Did you ever have one of those days when you should have stood in bed?"

Spock raised an eyebrow. "Standing in bed sounds like a pointless exercise."

"It's not pointless," said McCoy. "If I had stood in bed last night, none of this would be happening to me now."

"That is illogical," said Spock. "Your present would have occurred to you no matter what your posture in bed last night."

"You're as dense as a two-by-four," McCoy accused the Vulcan. "Have you listened to anything I said?"

"Excuse me," said Lisa. "I've got to get going. We don't always argue like this, do we?"

"No," answered Spock. "Under normal circumstances, we are too busy."

"Good." Lisa handed Spock the clipboard and hurried off. "See you around."

McCoy shook his head and sighed. "My luck has got to change sometime, doesn't it?"

"There is no such thing as luck," replied Spock. "It is illogical."

McCoy rubbed his eyes. "Let me see if I can get a straight answer out of you. Is there a booth where I can call home?"

The Vulcan pointed to an alcove in the corner. "Over there, I believe."

"Thank you," said McCoy with an exaggerated bow.

The medical student twisted his hands as he walked toward the communications booth. How was he going to phrase this to his father? He couldn't make it sound as if it was *his* idea to stay in San Francisco over the break. But he didn't want to explain exactly why he had volunteered.

He settled into the booth and looked at the screen. Even though there was no door on the booth, noise inhibitors blocked out the sounds from the recreation room.

"Computer," he said, "I'd like to call a number in Georgia." He gave the number and settled back in his chair.

"Your name and account?" asked the computer. McCoy answered with his name and his academy account. He still had plenty of credit to make calls, as he hardly made any.

McCoy twisted nervously in his seat as he waited to be connected. He still didn't know what he was going to say. When his father's lined, cheerful face appeared on the screen, he nearly began to cry.

"I have bad news, Dad," he blurted out.

"You didn't flunk out, did you?" his dad asked with concern.

"Not yet," answered McCoy. "But I can't come home over the winter break, at least not until the end of it."

McCoy's father looked even sadder than when he thought his son was flunking. "Oh, I see. Well, everybody will be disappointed. What have you got, some extra studies?"

"Not exactly." McCoy had never been good at lying, especially to his dad. It was a family trait to stick with the truth. "Dad, I got in trouble for doing something stupid. To make amends, I joined a service club, Disaster Relief, and we have training next week."

A smile creased his father's face. "Disaster relief can get pretty rough. You take care of yourself, Son. There will always be lots of other times we can be together."

"Yeah, I guess so." McCoy wasn't so sure about that. After medical school, Starfleet could ship him off to the farthest corner of the galaxy, and his dad wasn't getting any younger.

"As soon as the training is over," he promised, "I'll let you know if there's any chance of me getting home."

"Just do a good job, and make us proud of you." The older man must have seen something in his son's eyes, because he asked, "Are you happy there?"

"No, not really," admitted McCoy. "But I've made too many mistakes already, so I'm going to stick it out at the academy. I don't want to fall behind again."

"It doesn't matter where you finish the race," said his dad, "only that you finish it. Don't worry about us, we'll save you some catfish."

McCoy smiled. "Thanks, Dad. My love to everybody. Good-bye."

"Bye, Leonard." His dad smiled, but his lower lip quivered a bit.

The cadet turned off the computer, and the screen went blank. He sat staring at the dark phosphors for a moment, wondering if he would ever know what he really wanted. He hadn't gone home for years, so why should he be so upset about missing this trip? What did he really want—all of space, or a small town in Georgia?

It just seemed as if there wasn't enough time to do anything. Not enough time to study, to visit his family, or figure out where he was going with his life. How could someone even find the time to have a girlfriend?

His luck had to get better, decided McCoy. Despite what the Vulcan had said, he knew there was such a thing as luck. Right now, his was all bad.

Chapter
3

A week later, McCoy's luck still hadn't changed. He was crouched on the floor of a burning building, knee-deep in hot ashes. There was no fresh air, because he was breathing from a tank on his back. Searing flames lapped up the oxygen and pressure-cooked his padded fire suit.

The tricorder! he told himself. He could barely see in the thick smoke, even with his helmet and faceplate. The sweat was running down his back from the hot suit, and he just wanted to get out of there and jump in a lake.

Get the tricorder! his mind ordered. McCoy fumbled for the contraption on his utility belt—every movement was difficult with the thick gloves. He finally pulled the medical tricorder out and began scanning for life signs.

He found a life sign—weak enough to be a dying child—about fifteen meters away. The child was under a fallen metal oven, if that was possible. Anything was possible, McCoy told himself, in this hellish aftermath of a meteor striking a defenseless planet.

McCoy staggered to his feet in the heavy gear and ran for the spot where he detected the life sign. He again consulted his tricorder, and the readings were definite but fading. He had to act fast, and his only course was to try to move the teetering oven. It seemed to be pinning the child under fallen floorboards.

He grabbed the oven and tried to budge it. A twinge of protest from the muscles in his back made him realize that he wasn't strong enough. Then he remembered that he had help in the form of several exotic pieces of equipment.

McCoy took the forcefield brace out of his side pocket. The instrument was no bigger than a flashlight, but it could hold up a ceiling. It was overkill to use it to lift an oven, but there was no time to think of something better. He had to save that child!

With a twist, he set the device to what he hoped was enough outward force to move the oven about a meter. Unfortunately he didn't set it for a gradual release, and the forcefield bounced the oven onto its side. The sudden weight crushed the floorboards underneath, and the oven disappeared in a cloud of sparks and smoke.

McCoy gulped and peered into the crater where the life signs were. After waving away the smoke, he could see the girl! She was about ten years old and pinned under chunks of the wall. If she was alive, it was only barely—she looked unconscious.

He fought the temptation to check for a pulse—the tricorder said she was still alive, and he would save time

by believing it. As the flames roared all around him, the medic-in-training tried to remember the exact steps he had to take.

First he slapped a locator badge on the girl's chest, then he gave her a hypo with ten cc's of stimulant to survive the transporter. After doing that, McCoy backed away, stumbling, and touched the button on the side of his helmet.

"Alpha-nine to base!" he shouted, his own voice ringing in his ears. "One to beam up, critical! Locator one-zero-zero."

"Transporting," answered a businesslike voice. "She's very weak."

"Just get her," muttered McCoy. The last thing he wanted to hear was that the child had been lost in a transporter beam. That was the way he feared to go, and he hated those unnatural contraptions. Flames began to soar all around him, and McCoy scuttled on his hands and knees out of the burning building.

As he sprawled into the grass and looked up at the bright blue sky, he wondered if he had made a mistake. Actually, a lot of mistakes. Starfleet Academy was just one of them. He yanked off his helmet and breathed the damp air of San Francisco, and even it smelled good.

"Score seventy-five," announced Captain Raelius.

Despite the heavy suit, McCoy jumped to his feet. "But, sir, didn't I rescue the child?"

The dark-skinned, gray-haired woman gave him an icy glare. "Yes, but you destroyed our floor in there. On a real site, you could have taken out the entire floor with that stunt. Next time check the timing on the brace."

"Yes, sir."

Captain Raelius put her hands on her hips. "Now we've got to wait while our crew has to turn off the fire and resurrect the oven. Your overall time was also slow, Mr. McCoy, although you administered the hypo efficiently."

She glanced at the replay of his performance on her screen. "You still have to familiarize yourself better with the equipment. You passed, but it was a less than sterling performance."

McCoy still breathed a huge sigh of relief. "I just

didn't want to lose the survivor, especially in the transporter. Maybe it would help for me to see it done. Could I watch somebody else go through it?"

The captain nodded and opened up her communicator. "Raelius to Clayborne, how are the repairs coming?"

"We're almost done, sir." McCoy could hear scuffling footsteps over the tiny device. "All right, Captain, we're clear. You can ignite when ready."

Raelius nodded to the control tower in the center of the training yard. At once, the row of decrepit buildings burst into flames. Fingers of fire lashed out the open windows. Fortunately the entire structure was fireproof. It was still a very realistic simulation, thought McCoy. A little too realistic.

"Send the next one," ordered Captain Raelius into her communicator. She glanced at her screen. "That would be Cadet Spock, the Vulcan."

McCoy peered over the captain's shoulder to watch a lithe figure cut bravely through the flames. True, the Vulcan was wearing a fire suit, but it was as if he didn't even know fear of the flames. He stood calmly in the center of the burning building and consulted his tricorder.

"Nobody is expected to actually lift the oven," Raelius told McCoy. "So at least you had the right idea."

Satisfied with his readings, Spock strode through billows of smoke and into the kitchen. He swiftly located the robotic child under the floorboards, hung his tricorder on his belt, and moved toward the oven.

"He's going to try to lift it," said McCoy with a smile.

"Almost everyone does," remarked the captain.

But Spock didn't try to lift the fallen oven. With complete confidence, he bent down and picked up the oven as if it were a box of feather pillows. Then he carefully set it down in the most secure part of the room.

McCoy and Captain Raelius gaped at one another. "I heard they were strong," muttered the captain, "but that's *strong.*"

The Vulcan's movements were uncannily rapid and sure as he administered the hypo to the robot and put a locator badge on her chest. As calmly as if he were reporting the weather, Spock said, "Alpha-ten to base. One to beam up, critical but stable. Locator one-zero-zero."

"Transporting," replied the voice of the nonexistent chief. "Got her cleanly."

"Spock out." The Vulcan didn't run from the burning building as McCoy had—he calmly checked his tricorder to see if there were any other life-sign readings. Only when he was satisfied that the building was clear did he stroll into the sunlight.

"Well done!" said Captain Raelius. "Mr. Spock, you scored one hundred percent and set a record time for this exercise." She glanced at McCoy. "If you want to know how to do it, that's how you do it."

"Yeah," said McCoy thoughtfully. "Good job there, Spock."

The Vulcan looked matter-of-factly at the humans. "A satisfactory job, no more. I hope to improve upon it."

"You could say 'thanks,'" grumbled McCoy under his breath.

"Mr. McCoy," said Captain Raelius, "you have the

medic's course on bandaging and compression at eleven-hundred hours. Get some lunch, and we'll see you back here at fifteen hundred."

"Yes, sir," said McCoy. He trudged off wearily in the heavy fire suit.

After several hours of bandaging robots until his fingers were stiff, McCoy's luck took a turn for the worse. He reported back to Captain Raelius, who put him at the front of the line. His mouth gaping, McCoy stared at one of his worst nightmares—a long ladder that stretched upward into infinity.

Actually the ladder extended to a fifth-story window, but it sure looked like infinity. The narrow metal rails and rungs looked as flimsy as spiderwebs. He would almost rather join the cadets across the street, who were flying around with jetpacks on their backs.

The sight of the ladder brought back a childhood memory, when workers had left a ladder up to his family's roof. Being a dumb kid, he tried to climb it. He got most of the way and froze when the ladder began to creak. That creaking sound was the killer—it was the same thing that scared him about Ferris wheels.

In the roof escapade, they ended up having to call the police to rescue him. They might have to do that again, thought McCoy, because now he was supposed to climb five times that far. It couldn't possibly be safe way up there, creaking and swaying in the wind.

"Go on," said Captain Raelius at the base of the ladder. The ladder was attached to a hovercraft that looked sturdy enough, but McCoy had seen it flying only a few minutes ago. He didn't care that it was now parked sturdily on the ground. There was nothing in that fifth-floor window that he wanted to see.

"I don't suppose that medics can be excused from this exercise?" asked McCoy meekly.

"No exceptions," answered Raelius. "We have a man up there watching for you. All you have to do is climb the ladder, put the locator badge on the victim, and call for backup. In less than two minutes."

McCoy nodded bravely. At least he didn't have to wear a thick fire suit, only a protective helmet, first-aid kit, and rescue equipment. *Just a little climb up a ladder,* he told himself. *Pretend it's a steep set of stairs.*

He forced his legs to move, and he walked unsteadily onto the hovercraft. Taking a deep breath, he stepped upon the first rung. When nothing terrible happened, he kept going up, rung after rung. To his surprise, it wasn't too bad.

Then his backpack began to cut into his shoulders as he kept reaching higher. His utility belt, which had felt light on the ground, suddenly weighed him down like a ball and chain. His arms were already weary by the time he was level with the first floor, and he had four more to go!

McCoy was okay until he made the mistake of looking down. The ground and streets below him sloshed around like a pool of water. He found himself getting woozy, as if he were standing on a diving board in the hot sun, ready to dive in.

That's concrete down there! he told himself. McCoy forced himself to look upward, but that wasn't much better. The ladder still looked like gossamer threads that wouldn't hold a fly, and the open window looked so far away that it was only a rumor.

Also McCoy knew that he had to keep his legs moving, or he would blow the two-minute time limit. And he didn't want to have to do this again! With that thought in mind, he kept his legs moving one rung after another, but the only place he could stand to look was at his hands.

To look up was bad—to look down was terrible.

He supposed he was about halfway up the ladder, and he was getting into a rhythm with his climbing. Then that famous San Francisco wind started howling. A gust hit him and the ladder swayed and creaked.

McCoy hugged the metal rails with both arms, and he thought he could survive the wind. But the groaning of the ladder set his teeth to gnashing. McCoy forgot what he was doing and looked down. The ground didn't even look real anymore—it was like a map or a toy. The only reality was that he was swaying around on a creaky ladder fifty meters in the air!

Keep climbing! McCoy told himself. *There's an open window only a few meters ahead.*

Suddenly the window became more than a crazy goal, it became his salvation. He wasn't even thinking about the pretend victim on the fifth floor—he was thinking about saving himself and getting off this infernal ladder.

McCoy's legs began to pump all by themselves, and he kept climbing hand over hand, up and up. Only fear was making his body work, but it was doing a great job.

When he actually got close to the window, he was surprised to see a trainer gazing at him.

"Move it, Cadet," urged the trainer. "Your time limit is almost up."

McCoy was still thinking only about getting off the ladder as he scurried the last few meters. The wind was wailing at this height, and a seagull glided lazily past him. McCoy kept his eyes fixed on the welcoming window, looking nowhere else. Finally he vaulted headfirst through the open window and tumbled gratefully to the floor.

The trainer looked down at him with disgust. "You have ten seconds."

Without a moment to think, McCoy leapt to his feet and turned on his tricorder. He rapidly located the robotic dummy in a bedroom and rushed there. Counting off the seconds as he ran, he pulled a locator badge out of his pack and slapped it on the dummy's chest.

Then he snapped open his communicator. "Alpha-nine to base," he announced. "One victim found, unconscious. Request backup."

"You made it with one second to spare," said Captain Raelius. "Not well done, but done. Come on down."

McCoy sighed gratefully. He turned to the trainer and smiled. "How do I get out of here?"

"What do you mean, how do you get out of here? Down the ladder."

"*Down* the ladder?" gasped McCoy.

The trainer scowled. "Do you think there will be a lift or a transporter everywhere you go? In an emergency, you can't trust the lifts or transporters. So it's back down the ladder for you."

McCoy's shoulders slumped. This was going to be even worse than climbing up had been, because now he would have to look *down* to see where he was putting his feet. And the first step was going to be the hardest, as he had to back out the window and onto the ladder.

At that moment, the idea of quitting the Disaster Relief Service Club seemed very sensible. Even logical. But the trainer was right, too. There was no point learning to climb up a ladder if he couldn't also learn to climb down.

"Clamp your safety line to the top rung," said the trainer. "That will make you feel safer when you start down."

"Thanks." McCoy pulled the clamp of his safety line from the belt on his waist. The line was on a spring that loosened if pulled slowly but tightened if pulled quickly in an emergency. He did feel safer after he fastened the clamp to the top rung of the ladder.

Nevertheless, McCoy didn't like sticking his legs out the window and dangling them in space. He was very relieved once his feet finally landed on a rung and he could stand. He couldn't leave his safety clamp fastened to the top rung, so he unfastened it and started down, slowly and steadily.

McCoy wanted desperately to get to the ground, but he was in no hurry. He got back into a rhythm and began to feel as if he would survive this experience. He discovered that he could look at his feet and avoid looking at the woozy ground so far below. *He was going to make it!*

Aftershock

Suddenly the ladder jerked hard, and McCoy was tossed over the handrails. He lunged for the rung and held on while his legs swung loosely under the ladder. With his heart pounding, he fought to get a grip on the damp rung. Below him, people were running in confusion, or maybe it just looked that way from fifty meters in the air.

His fingers began to slip. "Help!" yelled McCoy.

Chapter
4

McCoy screwed his eyes shut, not wanting to watch himself hurtle toward the concrete. Then he realized that he wasn't falling yet, and he wouldn't fall until his fingers gave out. He tried to swing his legs to get his feet back on the ladder, but every movement weakened his grip.

All he could do was hang in the air and depend on his fingers, already numb from wrapping bandages. He kept trying to think about what he had done wrong. Had he made a wrong step? No, it seemed as if the ladder had jumped on its own, as if a giant had bumped into it. He always knew he couldn't trust these rickety contraptions.

McCoy grunted as he swung up and got a better grip with his right hand. "Help!" he shouted.

He heard the captain's voice on a bullhorn. "Hang in there, Cadet! There was a *real* earthquake, and it knocked out our instruments. But . . . who is that?"

Aftershock

McCoy heard a hissing noise, and he turned to see what had interrupted Captain Raelius. Flying straight toward him, standing erect in thin air, was a human rocket ship. He blinked in amazement until he realized that it was a cadet wearing a jetpack.

Suddenly he recognized the long brown hair streaming out from beneath the helmet. "Lisa!" he croaked.

The high-flying cadet said nothing—she just swooped ever closer. The noise from her jetpacks almost drowned out the pounding of his heart in his ears. Lisa looked like an angel as she hovered over him.

"Cadet Donald," warned the voice of Captain Raelius from below, "be very careful. The jetpack can't support both of you!"

"I know that," said Lisa grimly.

"Also, watch your fuel," added the captain. "Don't do anything hasty."

"Do something hasty!" shouted McCoy, as his grip slipped down to the first knuckle.

"Hold still!" With rockets shooting from her back, Lisa swerved dangerously close to him. She took her right hand off her controls, reached for his utility belt, and just missed it. Her motion nearly caused a collision, and she came within a millimeter of slamming into Mc-Coy's legs.

"Get away!" he yelled. "It's too dangerous!"

"Hold still," she told him. With her face set determinedly, Lisa again piloted her body toward McCoy. This time, she reached out and grabbed his belt, nearly tearing him off the ladder.

But he hung on as she fumbled for the clamp of his

safety line. He watched in amazement as she pulled out the line and slammed the clamp onto the nearest rung. Now he could let go and not fall to his death!

He grinned at the angelic Lisa as she swerved away on the jetpack. "Well done!" came a relieved voice from below. "Hang on, Mr. McCoy, as we lower you."

A few minutes later, McCoy was drinking a cup of hot broth from his own first-aid kit. Captain Raelius stood nearby, and the older lady looked apologetic.

"Who would have expected a real earthquake?" she asked.

"Well, San Francisco is famous for earthquakes," McCoy pointed out. "Was there any damage to the city?"

"Other than power interruptions, no. It was a mild temblor."

"It didn't feel mild on that ladder," said McCoy.

Raelius smiled. "We often have to work under conditions like that."

"Wonderful," McCoy said to himself.

"Under realistic conditions, you did very well," added the captain. "I'm giving you one hundred percent for this exercise. That should bring your score into the acceptable range for a medic."

"Then I can have the rest of the day off?" asked McCoy hopefully.

Raelius shook her head sadly. "I'm afraid not. Tonight you have a class in emergency field surgery."

"Great," muttered the cadet. "I nearly get killed twice today, and now I have a class in sawing off legs. Probably with no anesthetic."

"I'm sorry," said the captain. "This is a crash course."

"Sir, I would make one request. When we go to three-person teams, I'd like Lisa Donald and Spock with me. It's the least you can do to keep me alive."

Captain Raelius smiled and nodded. "I'll consider it."

After the incident with the ladder, McCoy's luck took a turn for the better. The second half of the training was devoted to teamwork, using a standard team of two diggers and a medic. With Lisa and Spock as his teammates, handling the hard stuff, McCoy had to do little more than aim his medical scanner or shoot a hypo.

Finally, seven days after the grueling training started, the members of Disaster Relief gathered with Captain Raelius and their trainers in the empty cafeteria. It was time for their induction into the service club.

With twelve hours of training every day, there hadn't been any time for fun. Plus everyone else on campus had gone home for winter break. So this induction was a welcome time to blow off steam.

Captain Raelius treated everyone to sparkling apple cider. "It was a tough training," she said, "especially with so many new members to the club. I wish to thank all the veteran members, who either took the training again or helped me do it."

The new members applauded the old members, many of whom had been trainers. McCoy looked around the room and estimated that the service club numbered about sixty. They didn't look especially brave or hardy, but they shared one important trait: They were all willing to risk their lives to save disaster victims.

At least, all of them were willing but one.

McCoy had never spent much time risking his life, although he knew it was part of serving in Starfleet. He hadn't planned on risking his life this early in his career, before he even got out of the academy. He didn't know how many dangers he could brave, or how many bleeding people he could save.

He looked around the room at the happy, smiling cadets. Did they realize what they were getting themselves into? He supposed that none of them really knew if they could run into a burning building until it came down to it. McCoy took some comfort from that thought as he sipped his apple juice.

Captain Raelius went on, "Our membership roll is higher now than it has been in five years. Our training didn't break any speed records, but we didn't lose anybody." She glanced at McCoy and smiled.

McCoy smiled back, just grateful that it was all over.

Captain Raelius raised her glass. "Let me welcome all of you to the greatest service club in the history of Starfleet Academy—Disaster Relief. Wherever you spend the rest of your careers, I want you to remember that you are part of this team. So I have a little surprise for you."

Raelius nodded to an aide standing by the door, and he rushed out. He returned a moment later pushing a clothing cart that was laden with jackets. The gray jackets had leather trim and beautiful patches showing a lightning bolt and the silhouette of two cadets carrying a stretcher.

"Our own jackets!" shouted someone.

"Yes," answered Raelius with a grin. "I've been thinking about doing this for a long time. After all, we're a team, so we need team jackets. I hope you like the patch, which I designed myself. We have lots of sizes, so form a line and get your jacket." There was enthusiastic applause for the faculty advisor.

"Isn't this exciting!" said Lisa Donald, standing beside McCoy.

McCoy smiled at Lisa. "Yes, it is. Thanks a lot for getting me through this in one piece."

"You're welcome," said Lisa with a bow. "And thank you for talking me into joining in the first place. As you promised, there was plenty of fresh air and exercise."

She nodded thoughtfully. "McCoy, I think you're going to make a good medic. You work fast and seem to know what you're doing."

"I'm not sure I do," answered McCoy. "The medical part comes naturally—it's the human side that's tough. What do you tell a child who has lost his parents in a disaster? What do you tell a person who is dying and can't be saved? They didn't teach us any of that."

Lisa shrugged sympathetically. "I don't think they can teach us that. You're very sensitive, McCoy. I like that."

Gazing at Lisa, McCoy suddenly got a brainstorm. She had a boyfriend, true, but her boyfriend was probably gone for winter break. He was planning to head home tomorrow, so tonight might be his only chance with Lisa.

"You're not leaving until tomorrow, are you?" he asked.

She shook her head. "I don't think I'm leaving. It's a long way to my home on Alpha Centauri. By the time

I got there, I would just have to come back. And it's so quiet in the dorm that I think I'll stay and get a head start on next semester's reading."

"You can't read on an empty stomach," said McCoy. "How about joining me for dinner?"

Lisa smiled. "Let's get our jackets, and I'll think about it."

McCoy was surprised when he put on his club jacket, because he actually liked it. Clothes didn't usually impress him, but this was a very handsome jacket. Plus it was warmly padded for those cool San Francisco nights. For the first time, McCoy felt proud and not nervous about being in the Disaster Relief Service Club.

Spock came up behind them and accepted a jacket. If possible, the Vulcan looked even more dour than usual.

"Spock," said McCoy, "this is supposed to be a happy occasion. Why aren't you happy?"

"I am satisfied with our training," answered the Vulcan. "However, that is no reason for unseemly displays of emotion."

"No, of course not," said McCoy. "You wouldn't want to offend anybody." He just shook his head, glad that most Vulcans in Starfleet served aboard the *Intrepid*. At least he would never have to serve with Spock. What a pain that would be.

"We've got to go somewhere and show off these jackets," he told Lisa. "What do you say?"

She smiled "Okay."

McCoy jabbed a victorious fist in the air. His luck indeed had changed. Tonight, a date with the lovely and brave Lisa. Tomorrow, off to see his family!

He looked around the cafeteria, wondering when they would be dismissed. Captain Raelius was deep in conversation with a Starfleet officer who had just entered the room. Both of them were looking at an electronic clipboard. Most of the cadets were still admiring their new jackets.

"Are we done?" asked McCoy.

"I believe not," answered Spock.

McCoy turned to see Captain Raelius stride to the front of the room. She put her hands up to quiet the cadets, and she looked as somber as Spock.

"Attention!" she snapped, stopping all noise cold. "You're going to be able to use your training sooner than we thought. The colony planet of Playamar has suffered severe and unexpected earthquakes that have liquified much of the coastal regions and river banks.

"With a high content of clay and sand in Playamar's soil, the liquefaction is having a terrible effect. It's toppling buildings and causing rifts and mudslides. Units are being flown in from all over the Federation to help the rescue effort. We leave in half an hour."

"Half an hour?" whispered McCoy in shock.

"Don't bring any personal items—we'll supply everything. Report to transporter room one."

"Transporters?" He looked helplessly at Lisa.

She shook her head. "You were right, McCoy."

He blinked at her. "I was?"

"Yes, you said we would be going to exotic places. You can't get much more exotic than Playamar."

"Move it out!" barked Captain Raelius.

Chapter
5

McCoy stared at his aunt Delia, a slim woman in her late fifties. She was wearing an apron and basting a turkey as she talked to him over the video link.

"I don't know where your dad is, Leonard. Can I have him call you back?"

The cadet's shoulders slumped. "No, Aunt Delia, that's all right. I'll be gone by the time he gets back. Just tell Dad I'm sorry, but I can't make it home over the break after all."

"Oh, you can't," said Delia. "That's too bad."

"But it's for a good cause," added McCoy, trying to sound upbeat. "I'm in the Disaster Relief Service Club, and we have to respond to an emergency."

"Well, be careful. We'll miss you."

"Thanks. Good-bye, Aunt Delia." The cadet closed the connection and slumped back in the seat of his comm booth. For the first time he realized that there were real sacrifices involved in a career in Starfleet. It sounded like fun and adventure, but one's personal life had to come second, after his duty.

McCoy wanted to save lives and do his duty, but he also wanted something like a normal life. Maybe that wasn't possible in Starfleet.

He stood up, picked up his new jacket, and left the comm booth. As he strolled across the campus green, he glanced at the lawn where the fateful football game had taken place. Until that day, he had thought that Starfleet Academy was about studies and exams, like any other school.

Now he realized that he had been kidding himself. All of Starfleet was about risking your life for other people, being part of a team, and putting duty before personal business. It was a sobering thought for a young man who was used to thinking mostly about himself.

Not only that, but the entrance to transporter room one loomed ahead of him. There was already a line of cadets, even though he was early. McCoy's heart started pounding as fast as it had been when he was dangling from the ladder.

Spock stood in line ahead of him, and Captain Raelius was checking off names. "McCoy, you room with Spock in four-twelve."

He blinked at her. "Room with Spock?"

"Yes," she answered. "You two were partners in training, and you'll be partners from here on out. We haven't got time to break in new teams. Lisa Donald will make the third in your team on Playamar, but she'll room somewhere else." The captain headed off to intercept two more cadets.

"We are boarding the *Nightingale,*" explained Spock. "She is a hospital ship, and they have converted some hospital rooms to crew quarters."

"Oh, great," muttered McCoy. "We'll be sleeping in a hospital room. If that's not an omen, I don't know what is."

Spock squinted slightly at him. "An omen? Do you mean the quaint custom of foretelling events by signs and portents? Most illogical."

"It's just an expression," said McCoy, getting testy. "Let's get one thing straight, Spock. I'm the medic on our team, and that makes me the boss. Understood?"

The Vulcan nodded curtly. "That is my understanding of the chain of command. Our mission is to save lives and relieve suffering. As the medic, it is logical that you can best direct our actions."

"And don't you forget it," snapped McCoy. "And this team is going to be run by *emotion*. Good old human emotions. We may do some illogical things from time to time, but the overriding concern is to save lives."

"We are in agreement," said Spock. "However, I will point out the logical course if it differs from yours. It would be negligent of me not to do so."

"I'm sure." McCoy looked up and saw the transporter operator motioning them toward the platform. He turned a skin color that was stranger than Spock's.

"Are you ill?" asked the Vulcan, taking the medic by the elbow.

McCoy winced. "Just head me toward the transporter. I'll deal with it."

Spock lifted an eyebrow. "Fear of transporters. Porta-brevaphobia. Most interesting."

"It's with good reason," said McCoy. "In med class, we've been studying about transporter accidents."

"Statistically unlikely," said the Vulcan.

If only to get away from the know-it-all Vulcan, McCoy puffed up his chest and jumped on the transporter platform. *Go ahead, let them scramble his molecules. What difference did it make after everything else that had happened to him lately?*

Spock stepped up on the pad beside him. "Transporters are the safest form of mass transit over short distances."

"I don't care," muttered McCoy. "They're unnatural."

McCoy nodded to the transporter operator, who said, "Energizing."

Holding his breath, McCoy watched the room dissolve all around him, only to be replaced by a room that was gleaming white and chrome. Emergency equipment and gurneys stood neatly off to the side, and there was room to transport an army of casualties.

Being in a medical facility relaxed him somewhat, and McCoy was able to walk off the transporter platform instead of run. A lieutenant checked him in, and he tried to stay two steps ahead of Spock. But the Vulcan took a few strides and caught up with him in the corridor.

Well, thought McCoy, there was no way to elude him—they were both going to the same place. "So which way?"

The Vulcan pointed. "Turbolift C to deck four. We are going in the correct direction."

The *Nightingale* had the look and feel of an empty ward in a sleek new hospital. Several of the numbered rooms had clear doors, yet he could see nothing but darkness beyond. There were empty nurses' stations, empty offices for support staff, empty laboratories. They would all be filled in a few hours.

The turbolift was large, built to hold gurneys full of patients. It felt odd riding on the huge lift with only Spock for company. When they got off on deck four, McCoy was relieved to find that it was a bit livelier.

Several people were loitering in the corridors, talking in low voices. Not all of them were Starfleet cadets. A group was playing cards in one of the empty nurses' stations, and a laboratory was in use. McCoy and Spock nodded to the others as they walked past.

They found room 412 without any problem. It had cots instead of hospital beds, a computer console, and uniforms in the closet. Otherwise, it was a hospital room. There were even curtains to separate one patient from another, but McCoy didn't think he would mind the privacy.

Spock looked with interest at the computer console. "If we are connected to the ship's computer, I can do some preliminary research on Playamar."

McCoy yawned. "I'm sure they'll tell us everything we need to know. I'll take the cot by the door."

"As you wish," answered Spock. He sat down at the computer.

McCoy took off his jacket and lay down on the cot

for a moment, just to make sure he could sleep on it. He never got a chance to decide, because he fell asleep instantly.

In McCoy's dream, a lovely young lady was leaning over him, about to kiss him. A wisp of her hair touched his cheek, and she gently woke him ... by tossing his jacket over his head. McCoy flailed at the jacket with his arms and sat up to see Lisa Donald smiling at him.

"Come on, you two," she scolded them, "you'll miss dinner. Didn't you hear the announcement?"

"No," answered McCoy. Spock was hunched over the computer and didn't appear to hear Lisa even now.

"Spock!" she called.

The Vulcan sat back in his chair and stared at his screen. "Fascinating."

"What is?" asked Lisa.

"The history of Playamar. It was originally settled as a colony for retired miners from all over the Federation. Now it has a diverse population of twelve million. All the precolonization studies showed that the geology of the planet was stable. They should not be having earthquakes."

"But they are," said McCoy. "Sometimes logic doesn't always work."

Spock nodded. "Logic can be false if you are missing information. Playamar was originally claimed by the Danai, who opposed Federation colonization. Eventually the Danai were admitted to the Federation and given another planet to colonize. They dropped their claims to

Playamar. I wonder if the Danai have more information than we do."

McCoy shook his head. "None of this makes any difference, Spock, and we're missing dinner."

Spock turned back to his computer. "Then I suggest you go."

"Fine. Come on, Lisa." McCoy stalked out of the room, and Lisa trailed after him.

Halfway down the corridor, Lisa said, "Go easy on Spock. I think you hurt his feelings."

"That's not even possible," grumbled McCoy. "That green-blooded robot doesn't have any feelings."

"I don't know about that. He is half human."

McCoy stopped dead in his tracks. "Are you telling me that Spock is *half human*? I don't believe it."

"His mother is human," answered Lisa. "She visited the academy not too long ago, and I know people who have met her. But Spock was raised Vulcan."

McCoy scowled. "Still there's no reason why he couldn't show a speck of humanity every now and then."

They entered a giant turbolift and were whisked to the cafeteria. Like the rest of the hospital ship, it was clean, white, and brightly lit. They got into line and were quickly served plenty of steaming, hearty food.

McCoy held his tray under his nose and took a whiff. "I'm liking this better and better."

"The *Nightingale* is famous for her food," said Lisa. "We're lucky. Of course, breakfast tomorrow may be our last meal here. We'll be down on the planet."

"That's right," said McCoy. "I may go back for seconds."

As they set their trays on a table and settled down to eat, Captain Raelius took the podium at the front of the room. She looked unusually stern and businesslike, but she was wearing her club jacket. All talk died to a hush.

"I hate to spoil your appetite," she began. "With so many of you here, I thought we should show this to you now. We received this vidlog a few minutes ago, and it will show you the conditions on Playamar."

McCoy started shoveling food into his mouth. If they were going to gross him out, he wanted to eat as much as he could first.

But the images that appeared on the overhead viewscreens were not gross. They were amazing! Stately buildings and homes stood sunk in mud and bizarrely tilted. Walls had fallen down, making people's homes look like dollhouses. Wherever there was water the damage was worse, because the land had actually liquified.

From the air, one could see farmland that had been shredded into deep grooves that ran all the way to the ocean. Great rivers had changed course by hundreds of kilometers. The bluffs overlooking Playamar's famous beaches had collapsed, turning homes into driftwood. It was disaster on a huge scale.

Then the scene shifted to the human misery. Diggers were extracting people from tilted and crushed buildings. Some people were trapped in what appeared to be quicksand. Hospitals were set up in fields, and some victims were lying in the open air.

McCoy set down his fork. He didn't feel like eating anymore.

A middle-aged man appeared on the screen. His uniform was so caked with mud that it was impossible to tell his rank.

"Lieutenant Commander Wynorski to Starfleet Command," he began. "I've been asked to evaluate the conditions on Playamar, and they're desperate. The scenes we've shown are only a taste of what is happening. The original temblor was bad enough, but the aftershocks have been just as bad. It has made rescue work very difficult."

He took a deep breath. "With so many aftershocks, the soil never has a chance to harden. Much of it is still like mud or quicksand. Buildings are unsafe; fissures and mudslides can appear anytime, anywhere. Ion storms and serious injuries make it dangerous to use the transporters.

"The rescue teams are very spread out. Some cities haven't even seen a rescue team yet. We need your help, but we insist that you use extreme caution. We don't need any more casualties. This is Lieutenant Commander Wynorski from Playamar. End transmission."

There was no sound in the cafeteria, except for somebody dropping his spoon. McCoy looked around and saw Spock standing in the doorway. The Vulcan crossed his arms and looked back at him.

For once, figured McCoy, he probably looked as gloomy as Spock.

Chapter
6

The next day, everybody in the shuttlebay of the *Nightingale* looked grim, except McCoy. He had to hide a smile. Owing to ion storms on Playamar, it was decided not to use transporters except in life-or-death emergencies. That meant taking a shuttlecraft down to the surface, which was fine with McCoy.

Lisa stood in front of him and Spock behind him in the waiting room. Through the lone window, they could see the crew loading medical supplies, survival gear, and food into three shuttlecrafts. Gamma team—McCoy, Lisa, and Spock—were scheduled for departure on one of the tiny vessels.

"I'm a little scared," whispered Lisa.

"You wouldn't be normal if you weren't," answered McCoy. He glanced back at Spock.

"Under the circumstances," said Spock, "caution is advisable."

Captain Raelius burst into the waiting room and motioned to them. "Gamma team, you're next. I'd like a word with you first. Despite the talent you three have, you're the only team of all new members. So be careful down there. Don't be heroes, just do your job."

They answered at once, "Yes, sir."

Captain Raelius gave them an encouraging smile. "You may be the first team to reach Sunshine Hamlet, but tell them that more will be along. Remember, first you distribute supplies and evacuate as many injured as you can. After that, you check out reports of people trapped."

"Yes, sir," answered McCoy.

"If your relief doesn't come in twenty-four hours, check with me. In an emergency, Command Post Thirty-nine is the closest backup to you."

She pressed a panel to open the door. "Shuttlecraft *Mead* is waiting. Happy hunting."

McCoy led his team out, and they crossed the grooved landing surface to the *Mead*. When McCoy ducked through the hatch, he saw that it was a personal craft with seating for eight, normally. For this trip, every spare centimeter was piled with boxes, gear, and supplies. They could barely squeeze into their three seats.

The pilot and copilot looked back at them. One was a lizardlike Saurian with a purple beak; the other was a huge Andorian with blue skin and long antennae.

"Welcome aboard," said the Saurian. "I've got the coordinates for Sunshine Hamlet. Does that sound like the right destination?"

McCoy fastened his safety belt. "That's what we were told."

"It's on the main continent," said the pilot, "where most of the trouble is. Hold on, we're getting clearance. Bay doors are opening. Prepare for launch."

A few seconds later, they streaked out of the shuttlebay so fast that McCoy was pinned back in his seat. After they gained some distance, he looked out the window to see the *Nightingale* for the first time. For a hospital ship, she was surprisingly sleek—with a single broad hull and twin nacelles. Miranda class, if he remembered correctly.

Then he turned his attention in the other direction to see a purple horizon fill the pilot's window. Playamar looked a bit like Earth, only everything was darker and lusher. The deserts were reddish clay, and they were ringed by olive green forests. There weren't many mountains and only two continents, surrounded by vast purple oceans.

Playamar looked like paradise. It had been, until recently. Most of the population lived near the oceans or the rivers, but that was the wrong place to live when there was liquefaction. With a name like Sunshine Hamlet, thought McCoy, the town was probably right on the beach.

The ride got bumpy when they hit the atmosphere, and flames streaked across the windows. He knew they had nothing to fear from reentry heat, because of their shielding, but it was still a spectacular sight. Lisa, who braved jetpacks and transporters with ease, curled up in her seat.

"Almost there," McCoy assured her.

She gave him a bemused smile. "You were a basket case in training, and now you're calm. What's your secret?"

"Now it's too late to worry," he said cheerfully.

They finally made it through reentry, and they could look out the windows again. As they zoomed closer to the land, they could see the ripe red soil and the verdant forests. They didn't see any settlements until they got closer to a large river. Then the land changed dramatically.

Vast stretches of farmland lay clawed and scratched as if attacked by a planet-size monster. Black crevices sliced hundreds of meters into the crust of the planet. In some places, it looked as if the land had melted and hardened, only to melt again.

The river had left its banks and split into wild washes and finger lakes. There was a path of devastation dozens of kilometers wide. A town on the old banks had been cut in pieces; its houses looked like toothpicks stuck in the mud.

"My gosh," said McCoy. "Is that it?"

"No," said the Saurian pilot. "That's Kiernan. Sunshine Hamlet must be where the river meets the sea."

"That is unfortunate," said Spock. "We can expect damage to be severe in a delta region."

Spock wasn't exaggerating. As they neared Sunshine Hamlet, it was impossible not to stare at the bizarre wreckage. It didn't even look real. One side of a street might be perfectly fine, and the other side was buried in a ditch a hundred meters deep.

Elegant office buildings and tiny cottages listed at odd angles. Mudslides had piled several houses together at the bottom of a canyon. The marina was destroyed, with a beautiful pier sunk in the harbor.

Bobbing on the ocean was a flotilla of sailboats, canoes, rowboats, anything that would float. Apparently many of the survivors had wisely chosen to escape to the sea. When the land was shaking, why not?

Their pilot steered the shuttlecraft toward a section of

gnomelike cottages on the outskirts of town. It was about the only neighborhood still standing, and McCoy could see a large crowd of people down there. When they spotted the shuttlecraft, they surged toward it like a swarm of ants.

"Plenty of people here," said the Saurian. "Want to set down?"

McCoy found himself glancing at Spock.

"This section of town would appear to be bedrock," the Vulcan pointed out. "If it was not the safest place, they would not be gathered here."

"Can you set us down?" McCoy asked. He took a deep breath, remembering that on this mission, he was the person in charge.

"You could land in that wide street," said the Andorian. "But there's a crack down the middle of it."

"I'll only need half of it." Without hesitation, the little Saurian banked the shuttlecraft toward a boulevard that was sliced in half by a black fissure. McCoy closed his eyes, certain they would crash.

After a few bumps, the shuttlecraft came to a stop. McCoy looked out the starboard window and saw a yawning chasm that seemed to have no bottom. Then he turned to port and saw a mass of humanity surging toward them. It was hard to say which was more frightening!

He pointed at his comrades. "Spock and Lisa, start unloading. I'll try to talk to them." The cadets nodded in accord.

The Saurian popped the hatch, and McCoy pushed his way past everyone to get out first.

When he saw a stampede of angry survivors headed his way, McCoy nearly ducked back into the craft. Most of them *looked* human, but it was hard to tell, they were so covered with grime. He zipped up his jacket and waved his hands to stop them.

"Stop!" he called. "We have supplies! We have food! We are here to evacuate the injured!"

The surly crowd stopped and stared at him with frightened eyes. "Who are you?" asked a dazed survivor. "You're just a kid!"

McCoy pointed to the patch on his jacket. "I'm part of the relief team from Starfleet, and I'm a medic. More importantly, I'm here to help you. Now move back, form an orderly line, and let these people unload your supplies."

The people of Sunshine Hamlet gulped sheepishly and stepped back. Spock, Lisa, and the shuttlecraft crew were unloading boxes as quickly as they could. They would be unloaded in minutes, thought McCoy, but handing out the food and supplies was going to take longer.

He turned to the nearest local. "Where are the injured people? We can evacuate some of them. If it's life or death, we can transport them."

"Take us all!" begged the man, gripping McCoy's collar. Others wailed the same plea and pressed forward. Soon the panicked crowd was pushing McCoy toward the shuttlecraft, and he was worried that they would push the vessel into the chasm.

"Stop unloading!" he shouted. "Take off! Take off!"

That stopped the crowd, and so did Lisa's sharp voice.

"You're right!" she shouted. "Let's take our supplies somewhere they deserve it!"

"We only want some help!" wailed an older woman.

"And we're here to give it to you," answered McCoy. "But you've got to be patient. The sooner you let the shuttlecraft leave, the sooner it can come back with *more* supplies. We're only the first relief team—there will be more."

"When?"

"Tomorrow!" He had no idea if that was true, but Captain Raelius had promised relief in twenty-four hours. By the looks of this mob, they were going to need it. And these people were the ones in good condition.

The survivors backed up and began milling around. A small man with a beard came forward. He had dried blood all over his clothes, but he didn't appear to be injured.

"Did you ask about the wounded?" he said hoarsely.

"Yes," said McCoy. "Are you a doctor?"

The man nodded. "Dr. Whelan. It's too late for some, but we do have many who could be saved."

"'Is your water supply safe?" asked McCoy.

He nodded. "For the moment, the wells around here are working. We are boiling the water, and we have some chemicals to add."

"All right." McCoy glanced around and saw his comrades dispensing food and supplies to the waiting throng. Everything was as under control as it was going to be.

"Lead on." McCoy followed the little man to the largest house that was still standing. Like the smaller cottages, it had picturesque gables and a shingled roof that seemed to be out of a fairy tale. The architecture of Sunshine Hamlet was definitely whimsical. They were lucky they had built at least a few houses on bedrock.

"Did you ever have earthquakes before?" he asked Dr. Whelan.

The little man shook his head. "Never before. They told us it wasn't likely. There were no serious fault lines."

Just as Spock had said, thought McCoy. With a worried glance at the cracked doorway, he stepped into the house. Injured people were lying everywhere—in cots, on couches, scrunched up in corners. A handful of medical workers were doing the best they could with makeshift supplies and equipment.

McCoy swallowed hard and took a stack of locator badges out of his pocket. He turned to the doctor. "You must know which ones are critical. I mean, the ones who won't make it without immediate attention."

"Yes, I do."

McCoy handed him a stack of locator badges. "We don't want to use the transporters for everyone because of the ion storms, but we can transport the ones who are desperate. Just put a badge on them and mark down the numbers you use."

"Yes, I will!" said the doctor gratefully.

He hurried off, leaving McCoy to stroll through the rooms of the field hospital. The medic was looking for walking wounded, eight casualties who could follow him back to the shuttlecraft. He finally settled on four children and four adults with a variety of broken bones and head injuries.

By the time McCoy had organized his small group, the doctor had finished tagging the critical cases. He handed McCoy a list of the badges.

"There are twenty-two," he said sheepishly. "Is that too many?"

"No, it's fine," said McCoy. He opened his communicator. "Gamma team to *Nightingale.* We have twenty-two, critical condition, to transport immediately."

"Acknowledged," came the reply. "It's looking safe at the moment, but we have to stop at the first sign of an ion storm."

"Understood." McCoy gave the transporter chief the badge numbers. "Transport when ready."

All around the makeshift hospital, unconscious victims started to disappear in clouds of glimmering light. The other injured people seemed to enjoy the spectacle, and there was laughter and the sound of hope in the room.

McCoy looked at his eight patients, then turned to the doctor. "I'm going to take these people to the shuttlecraft. You should send some able-bodied people to our landing site, to bring back medical supplies."

"I'll be right there," answered Dr. Whelan. "Thank you for coming. Please excuse the way our people acted. They have been put through a nightmare."

"I can believe it," said McCoy. "But I can't believe nobody got here before us."

"Oh, others came here to make reports," said the doctor. "They just didn't stay. You'll see why." The little man turned to an assistant and started issuing orders.

McCoy shivered in the big, cold house. He ushered his charges out the door, through the wrecked neighborhood, back to the shuttlecraft. Spock, Lisa, and the two-man crew had already dispensed all of the food and were working on the supplies. The mob wasn't unruly any-more, and there was orderly cooperation.

McCoy waved to his comrades. "Dr. Whelan is going to the shuttlecraft for medical supplies. Here are your eight passengers to take back."

"Right this way," said the tall Andorian. He made sure the hatch was open, and he personally guided each of the eight injured people into the shuttlecraft. Then he went in after them.

The Saurian turned to McCoy and held out a clawlike hand. The human gripped it warmly. "We've got to be going," said the Saurian. "Take care of yourselves."

"Tell Starfleet about all these people, and the ones on the boats!" McCoy waved his hands out to sea. "You might need to do an old-fashioned airlift for them."

"We'll tell them." The pilot waved to Lisa and Spock, then he ducked into his shuttlecraft.

The three members of Disaster Relief pushed the crowd back to make room for the takeoff. They had barely cleared a path when the *Mead* zoomed off into the azure skies. Within seconds it was gone, and there was a frightened murmur in the crowd. It was as if all their hope had gone with the shuttlecraft.

Lisa let out a sigh. "It's just us now, and there are so many of them to help."

"The transporters are working at the moment," said McCoy. "We transported twenty-two criticals out."

Spock nodded with approval. "We have fulfilled our first two objectives—we delivered supplies and evacuated the injured. We should try to find individuals who are trapped and need immediate help."

McCoy nodded. "Okay, let's ask around."

Suddenly there came a low roar from the depths of Playamar, and the ground beneath McCoy's feet began to pitch and roll. It bucked like a trampoline, and McCoy staggered toward the gaping chasm.

Somebody screamed, "Aftershock!"

Chapter
7

McCoy threw himself to the ground and tried to scramble away from the gorge. But the earth was pitching and rolling underneath him, and he couldn't control his movements. He leg swung over the crevice, and the cement began to crumble underneath him!

Then a strong hand gripped his arm and dragged him back to level land. Before he could catch his breath, the shaking stopped. McCoy looked up and saw Spock lying on the ground beside him. The Vulcan slowly removed his hand from McCoy's arm.

"Thanks," breathed the medic.

"Gratitude is not required," said Spock. Even the Vulcan sounded out of breath.

"Lisa!" called McCoy.

She was wrapped around a box of medical equipment. "I'm okay. Was *that* an aftershock? It felt like a foreshock."

"That was an aftershock." A muscular man with a bushy red beard strode toward them. "That's why waiting to be rescued is so terrible for us. The aftershocks are constant, and we never feel safe. We can't leave this spot, and those people on the boats can't come back to land."

Spock took his tricorder off his belt and started taking measurements.

"Any casualties?" asked McCoy.

"Unknown," said Spock. "I am not scanning for casualties."

"Well, what are you scanning for?"

"The cause of the aftershocks. They should not be happening."

McCoy shook his head with frustration. "That's not our job, Spock. Didn't Captain Raelius tell us to just do our job?"

"Saving lives is our mission," answered the Vulcan. "Until these aftershocks stop, our success will be limited."

"He's right," said the man with the red beard. "There are a lot of places we can't get to because of the aftershocks."

"Okay," said McCoy. "Is there anybody still trapped? Anybody you people couldn't rescue?"

"Yes!" said the man. "There are two people trapped nearby in a house at the bottom of a fissure. We were there when we heard about your landing. We couldn't get to them, but we heard a voice."

McCoy looked around. Dr. Whelan had shown up and was taking charge of the medical supplies. Everything they had brought to the planet had been absorbed into the restless crowd, but it seemed like so little. What they really needed to do was get these people off the planet.

The wind picked up, blowing some dust into Mc-Coy's eyes.

"That is odd," said Spock. "We are experiencing an ion storm."

McCoy rubbed his eyes. "What's odd about that? We were warned about the ion storms."

"If the aftershocks and ion storms are this close together, there could be some connection."

"Come on," said McCoy, picking up a coil of rope. "Grab our equipment, and let's get going. Lead on—what did you say your name is?"

"Berthold," answered the big man. He motioned to three other locals to follow him, and they opened a path through the crowd. While McCoy and Lisa grabbed the backpacks, Spock hoisted the three jetpacks over his shoulder.

"You don't need all three of those," said McCoy. "I'm not wearing one."

"Perhaps not," said Spock. "But I will take all three."

After five minutes, they were sliding on their rear ends down a slick mud bank. It was all McCoy could do to avoid the roots and rocks; it was pointless to worry about getting dirty. By the time he collapsed into a flue of mud at the bottom, he was totally covered.

Berthold pulled him out of the muck, and they both helped Lisa. Then came Spock, walking most of the way down. "We have left the bedrock," he warned. "This area is subject to liquefaction."

Aftershock

"Let's cable ourselves together," said McCoy. "Five-meter intervals." Neither Lisa nor Spock argued with the order as they pulled their safety lines out. After adjusting the length, Lisa cabled to McCoy's waist, while Spock cabled to hers.

Berthold was laughing. "Believe me, if the aftershocks want you, they will get you. Those won't help."

"We believe in teamwork," said McCoy. He glanced at Lisa, and she gave him an encouraging smile.

The rescuers wound their way through a glade of trees, many of them broken and uprooted. They passed crushed houses and a playground under mud. Berthold and his people threw tree trunks over the most dangerous spots, so McCoy often found himself skittering across a muddy log. Birds shrieked as they flitted among the shattered trees.

Finally they came to a road and a roaring waterfall that pounded down from a bluff high overhead. The road was crumpled like an accordion, but one side of it had some intact cottages. There was a heavy mist in the air, which only added to the feeling of dampness and misery.

"Down there!" Berthold said. He pointed into the gorge where tons of water were plunging. "Careful, the waterfall wasn't here two days ago."

McCoy gazed up at the vertical river, marveling at the sheer force of it. He couldn't imagine that it had suddenly appeared, but there it was, slicing through the land with a vengeance.

Spock was the first to get out his tricorder, and he walked perilously close to the edge of the gorge. Lisa and McCoy had to follow, because they were roped together. The medic began to wonder about the wisdom of that order.

"I detect life signs, two of them," said the Vulcan.

McCoy got brave enough to step beside Spock and peer into the depths. Twenty meters below them, a tiny cottage rested on a ledge of mud and roots. The ground under the building had flattened like a pancake, dropping it in one piece. It looked like a bird's nest trembling in the wind.

"We must act quickly," said Spock. "The ground on which we are standing could erode any moment."

McCoy turned to Berthold. "Have you lowered lines down to them?"

"No, they are trapped under debris. They can't get out of the house. We heard voices before, but not for a while."

Everyone looked at McCoy, waiting for him to make a decision. No doubt Spock had an opinion, so McCoy knew that he had better get his orders out quickly. But what were his orders?

"We need to get down there," he said. "But where can we attach a line in this mud?"

"That is a problem," agreed Spock.

"Give me a jetpack," said Lisa. She tossed off her backpack and some heavy items on her belt. Before McCoy realized that she was serious, Spock handed her a jetpack.

"Wait, you can't," he said.

"Yes, I can," answered Lisa. She strapped the flying device to her back. "There's plenty of room to land down there. Then it's just a matter of getting into the house and sizing up the situation."

"Under these conditions, it is unwise to be tied to each other." Spock took his clasp off Lisa's waist.

Lisa removed her line from McCoy's waist and gave him a smile. "I don't think you want to come down there with me, do you, McCoy?"

"No, but somebody has got to go with you," he said worriedly. He picked up a jetpack. "Let me see, the right hand is the stick, and the left hand is the throttle?"

"That is correct," answered Spock. "However, I will accompany her. We have the jetpacks, but I need a rope for the victims."

McCoy gave him the coil, and Spock handed one end to Berthold. "Would you secure that."

"Yes, sir," answered the local man. He and his crew took the thick line and dashed toward an outcropping of boulders.

McCoy opened his tricorder and took life-sign readings. Yes, the two victims were still alive. "Don't be heroes," he told Lisa and Spock. "Just slap those locator badges on them and get out of there. And keep in touch with me."

Spock started the engines on his back and glanced in the direction of Berthold and his people. The big man waved from the rocks, and Spock shot off into the sky like a Roman candle. He hovered over the waterfall for a moment, looking like some giant bird in a prehistoric world.

Lisa quickly followed him into the dark blue sky. McCoy watched in amazement as the two humanoids

began to descend into the chasm with noisy bursts from their thrusters. He already began to worry about how much fuel they were burning.

He peered anxiously over the lip of the gorge and watched tensely as Spock and Lisa dropped toward the roof of the cottage. The roof responded with uneasy groaning sounds, and part of it buckled!

McCoy caught his breath as he thought Spock would fall into the hole. But the Vulcan remained calm and dropped the rope through the hole in the roof. The brave pair remained tense for several seconds, ready to escape to the air if anything happened.

When nothing happened they turned off their jets and slid down the roof to the muddy ground. McCoy lost sight of them, and he nearly fell into the crevice trying to find them. Then he heard glass smashing, and he figured they were entering through a window. He took out his communicator.

What seemed like an eternity passed, and McCoy fought the temptation to contact them. He had plenty of time to fasten the jetpack to his back, although he hardly expected to use it. Finally his communicator chirped, and he snapped it open. "McCoy here."

"We're inside," said Lisa, breathing hard. "There are two women. They're both conscious, but one has a broken leg and possible internal injuries. Spock is moving the fallen beams and tying the rope to them."

"What about transporting them?" asked McCoy.

"We checked. The *Nightingale* isn't transporting after that last ion storm. It's up to us. Don't worry, we've already tied the rope to their arms, and Spock has them clear of the debris."

Suddenly there came the sickening sound of wood splintering and cracking.

"Oh, no . . ." shouted Lisa.

"Lisa! Lisa!" shouted McCoy, but the communication was dead.

On his hands and knees, McCoy slid across the slippery mud to the lip of the chasm. He peered down, expecting the worst, and he saw it. The constant seepage of water had liquified the soil, and the ledge was breaking apart! With awful groaning and cracking sounds, the cottage slipped toward the abyss.

"No!" cried McCoy, but he was powerless to save his friends trapped inside.

Chapter
8

McCoy was about to close his eyes, unable to watch Lisa, Spock, and the survivors die. Suddenly an explosion ripped the roof off the cottage and sent debris flying toward him. He covered his head but managed to keep watching through a crack in his fingers.

As the cottage slid toward the churning waterfall, Lisa and Spock burst through the hole in the roof. Their jet-packs blasted smoke, but they were trying to carry the injured victims at the same time. The extra weight made their flight erratic.

Their feet had barely cleared the roof when the house jerked like a crashing wave and plummeted into the waterfall. In a second, it was smashed into driftwood. The flyers couldn't keep aloft for more than a few seconds with their precious cargo, and they dropped to the crumbling ledge.

McCoy jumped to his feet and waved at Berthold and his crew. "Start pulling them up! Slowly!"

The locals dug in and began pulling on the rope. McCoy leaned over the edge and saw the survivors being dragged through the mud. He wished there was a better way to get them out, but at least they were alive.

Lisa and Spock flew out of the gorge and landed on the rim near McCoy. Lisa was beaming with a combination of fear, excitement, and pride. Spock looked slightly winded but as calm as if he did this kind of thing every day.

McCoy felt like bawling them out for taking risks. Instead he said, "I don't think you're supposed to use the forcefield braces like that."

Lisa smiled and promptly grabbed the rope. They all began to haul on the rope, easing the injured women up the slope. Spock leaned over the edge and lifted them the last few meters.

It was a mother and a daughter, and they appeared to be more in shock than anything else. McCoy ran a scan for internal injuries. When he found none, he set the daughter's broken leg with a splint and gave the mother a hypo for shock.

The locals appeared with stretchers, and they took charge of the injured women. They thanked the rescuers profusely, but they were anxious to get back to the safety of the bedrock. McCoy couldn't blame them.

He looked around at the cockeyed planet that had been a paradise only a few days ago. There was so much to be done in this one town that it was overwhelming. Most of the town was impassable, a swamp—but they had to keep looking for survivors. How could they even get around in this deadly quagmire?

The answer was strapped to McCoy's back, but he didn't want to think about it. "Shall we walk down the road a ways?"

Spock turned to look at the crinkled road, which was slashed with streams and fissures. "Walking is most illogical."

Lisa put McCoy's hands on his jetpack controls. "Come on, it's really quite simple. The control stick is here, and the throttle is there. I saw you doing this in training."

"Just one flight," protested McCoy. "That was all I had time for. You guys go along. I'll walk."

"Here," she said, "you start it like this." She pushed the starter button, and the tiny jet engines roared to life.

"I don't want to!" yelled McCoy.

Before he could turn off the engines, the ground moved and knocked him off balance. *Aftershock!* he thought in panic. As he staggered down the slippery hill toward the fissure, his hand cranked the throttle on the jetpack. He shot twenty meters into the air, leaving his stomach and most of his senses down below.

But McCoy's reflexes were good, and he didn't panic. He knew there was nothing but safety straight up, so he kept an even keel as he let up on the throttle. With the jets roaring in his ears, he slowed to a hover. It was safe in the air over Playamar, he told himself, with most of the trees and buildings already knocked down.

McCoy looked down to see the aftershock still going on. As the ground shimmied and shook, water flowed in

and turned it into mush. Trees and buildings tumbled over, tilted, or cracked apart in slow-motion devastation.

By the time Lisa and Spock joined him in the air, the aftershock was over. There was nothing left but the shrieking of frightened birds and the thud of walls collapsing further.

Spock put his jetpack on autopilot and whipped open his tricorder. In a few seconds, he had seen all he needed. "Another ion storm," he reported.

"What about survivors?" asked McCoy. It was strange having a conversation in midair, but it was safer than being on the ground.

Spock nodded in the direction of the marina, the hardest hit area of Sunshine Hamlet. The latest aftershock had turned it into a giant pool of quivering sand. "I am picking up life signs in that direction," said the Vulcan.

McCoy gulped and looked up. "You lead, we'll follow."

They zoomed over the devastated city, gazing at a panorama of ruin. From the air, Sunshine Hamlet looked like a sand castle that had been struck by a wave—dirty, misshapen, crumbling.

McCoy would have feared that everyone was dead were it not for the hundreds of boats bobbing offshore, plus the people clinging to the bedrock. He sighed and concentrated on their destination.

There was little left of the marina except for sunken boats, tumbled buildings, and sand. Sand covered everything. Ahead of him, Spock swerved toward what looked like a fountain, and Lisa followed him without hesitation.

Was he going to land? wondered McCoy. The medic

had been worried about taking to the air—now he was worried about landing.

He looked toward the ocean and saw a small motor-boat steaming his way. The people on the flotilla of boats seemed to be watching the motorboat, as if it was an envoy from the boat people to the flying people. McCoy dipped cautiously toward the water, only getting low enough to hear what the pilot was yelling.

"Rescue us!" shouted the man. He cut his engine. "Take us with you!"

"I'm not going anywhere," growled McCoy. "More rescuers will be coming with food and supplies, so be patient. Do you have badly injured among you?"

"A few," answered the man in the boat.

McCoy held his breath and dropped lower. With his jets spraying water off the top of the waves, he tossed a bundle of locator badges into the open boat. When he saw his toss was good, he shot back up to safer heights.

He shouted down, "I'm a medic, so do what I say. Put those badges on people who are in critical condition, near death. It's dangerous to transport with these ion storms, so we're only transporting the criticals. If you have communicators, you can contact a hospital ship or-biting us—the *Nightingale*."

The man in the boat nodded. "Yes, yes! We have been in contact with them. Thank you!" He pointed to the spot inland where Spock and Lisa had landed. "Tell your friends to be careful in the pneumotubes."

"What are pneumotubes?"

"Our transit system. I'm sure there are people trapped down there, but we had no way to get them out."

"Thanks for the warning." McCoy waved, and the man gunned his engine and roared off into the choppy purple sea. He swung around and headed toward land in search of his comrades. He didn't want to land, but maybe they had better land and conserve fuel, or they might be trapped out there.

Spock and Lisa had found a fairly level place to set down, on a metal plate in the middle of a sandy street. The fountain was nearby. McCoy dropped down and tried to land on the plate, but he missed by two meters and landed in the sand—up to his waist!

McCoy flailed about in the wet, gooey sand, and he sunk up to his chest! He had never been in quicksand, but it couldn't be much worse than this. His jetpack pulled him off balance, and he sunk up to his chin. He was going to drown!

"On your back!" shouted Lisa. "Float!"

Float! He had two jets strapped to his back—he couldn't float. The quicksand flowed over his ears and up to his nose. He started holding his breath, going down. . . .

Suddenly a piece of rope slapped him in the face, and he reached desperately and grabbed it. The rope started to slip through his grimy fingers as Spock pulled on his end. With a surge of fear, McCoy gripped it, and the Vulcan yanked him out of the sand.

McCoy held on as he skidded mouth-first through the muck to the metal plate, which, he realized, was the top of a building. They lifted him out and set him on his stomach, and he coughed out sand and water for several moments.

"Liquefaction," explained Spock. "We must find a way to stop these aftershocks."

"No kidding," croaked McCoy. "Thanks for pulling me out of there." He staggered to his feet.

"Are you sure you're okay?" asked Lisa.

"No, I'd rather be sitting at home in a bathtub, my stomach full of turkey," growled McCoy. "New Year's Eve is only two days away. I wonder if we'll live to see it."

Spock totally ignored him and aimed his tricorder in the direction of the fountain. "The life signs are this way."

Warily, McCoy followed Spock, while Lisa moved behind him. He could tell she was keeping an eye on him, and he appreciated the protection. McCoy was still a little shaky from his brush with death. They padded carefully along solid materials such as cement, rock, and metal.

Walking on top of a wall reminded McCoy of childhood games when he walked the curb and tried not to fall. Only this time falling was dangerous. He kept his hand on his starter switch, ready to zoom into the sky rather than fall into the deadly sand.

As he got closer to the huge fountain, he saw that it wasn't really a fountain. It looked like something from a water park—a ring of circular slides pointed downward into a hole in the ground. There was a lip on each slide for easy entry, and these lips made the slides look like petals on a giant flower.

"They're called pneumotubes," said McCoy.

Spock nodded. "Individual public transportation. Most commendable." He studied his tricorder. "I detect fourteen life signs approximately ninety meters below us."

"Are you sure they're alive?" asked Lisa.

The Vulcan stepped toward the pneumotube entrance. "They are alive, but they are trapped in tubes running through the ocean."

"Can you get a fix for the transporter?" asked McCoy.

"Not from here. Actually it is to their advantage to be trapped under water, as the shifting land would have crushed the tubes. We must act quickly."

Spock picked up a shiny pad from the ground. It was about the size of a beach towel, and McCoy saw that the plaza was littered with them.

"I believe that a rider is supposed to recline on this pad," said Spock. "Then he is drawn through the tubes via manipulation of air pressure. One might attain considerable speed. However, we cannot use them under the circumstances." The Vulcan started toward the closest pneumotube.

"Spock!" called McCoy, "you're not going down there, are you?"

The Vulcan tied one end of his rope to the petal portion of the tube. "To take an accurate reading, I have no choice but to get closer. The descent will be slow, as the pneumatic equipment is not working."

"What about flooding?" asked McCoy.

"At the first sign of danger, we'll come back up," said Lisa. "'We've got to check on them."

"Hang on." McCoy opened his communicator and reported, "Gamma team to *Nightingale*."

"Go ahead, Gamma, this is Chief Henshaw."

"We have distributed locator badges to the people in the boats off Sunshine Hamlet. They will be calling you to transport their critical cases."

"That's all we're transporting, critical cases," answered the transporter chief.

McCoy glanced at the determined Vulcan and the equally determined woman. "We are going down into an underground transportation system. Can you track my signal in case we need to transport quickly?"

"Not with your locator badge," said the chief. "But if you keep your communicator with you, I can track your coordinates."

"Thank you. Gamma out."

Aftershock

Spock climbed upon the petal, dropped the rope down the pneumotube, and turned on a light on his belt. Within seconds he vanished into the darkness. McCoy peered down and could see the bobbing light for a few meters, then it vanished, too. Lisa slipped in after Spock, and the tube swallowed her as well.

McCoy took a deep breath and cursed James T. Kirk for landing him in this mess. He climbed upon the petal and found it grimy and dirty. As he edged himself down the slide, he realized that it would be slow going without the pneumatics and slick pads.

Even with a light on his belt, it was dark, dirty, and confining in the broken tunnel. He felt as if he was crawling into an old tomb.

McCoy didn't know how far they had sunk into the pit. It felt like a hundred meters, but maybe it was only ten. Finally he heard Spock's voice echoing up through the darkness. "I have stopped at an obstruction. I will attempt to dislodge it with a forcefield brace."

"Be careful," said McCoy. But the words had no sooner left his mouth than the pneumotube began to shake. McCoy rattled around inside the tube, and chunks of dirt tumbled down upon his head.

"Aftershock!" he shouted. After he said the dreaded word, the shaking abruptly stopped.

"It wasn't an aftershock," said Lisa. "It was Spock setting off the forcefield brace."

"Wow, it felt just like an aftershock!"

After a few moments, Spock's voice came up from below. "That is a brilliant observation, McCoy."

The medic blinked in surprise. "Did you get hit in the head, Spock?"

"No. I am taking a tricorder reading, and there is a miniature ion storm occurring inside this tube."

McCoy rubbed dirt out of his eyes. "Spock, what is this thing you have for ion storms? What about the survivors? Can we get to them?"

"We cannot rescue them, because this tube is still blocked. But I have pinpointed their coordinates, and we could transport them when it is safe. We must return to the ship immediately and talk to Captain Raelius."

"Captain Raelius!" snapped McCoy. "Let's just do our job and leave the captain alone."

"We may be able to stop the aftershocks."

"Stop the aftershocks? Are you kidding me?"

"Vulcans do not kid," came the solemn reply. "Nor do we lie. We must return to the surface and transport immediately back to the *Nightingale.*"

McCoy growled, "Come on, we're cadets, not engineers. Let somebody else figure out the aftershocks, and that's an order."

He heard Spock's communicator snap open and beep. "As a cadet, I am still a civilian. If necessary, I will request to transport right now."

"Don't you dare, you green-skinned mannequin!"

"You two, stop fighting!" ordered Lisa. She looked up at McCoy, and he could see her dirty face in the beam of his light. "McCoy, you're the boss, but if Spock knows something about these aftershocks, we ought to report it."

"Let's get back to the surface," said McCoy, "and he can tell me first."

Chapter
9

An hour later there was a break in the ion storms, and hundreds of people from Playamar were beamed to the *Nightingale*. They included people trapped in the pneumotubes, critical cases from the boats, plus McCoy, Spock, and Lisa.

The cadets found Captain Raelius in the shuttlebay, where she was still busy organizing the relief effort.

She scowled at them. "This had better be good, or I might accuse you of deserting your post."

"Can we talk privately, Captain?" asked McCoy. "It's sensitive information."

The captain looked with a puzzled expression from McCoy to Lisa, then Spock. She saw that the young cadets were serious, and she nodded. After assigning a lieutenant to take over for her, she led them into a small briefing room.

"Talk quickly," she said.

McCoy looked at Spock, and the Vulcan began, "We noticed that the aftershocks were always followed by ion storms."

"We noticed that, too," said Raelius. "Do you have a theory?"

"Yes," said the Vulcan. "We were underground, and I used a forcefield brace to loosen some debris. It was Cadet McCoy who observed that the effect was very much like an aftershock. I took a reading and noticed that ion levels were higher. Increased ion activity is a known by-product of forcefields."

Raelius frowned thoughtfully. "So you think the aftershocks are caused by forcefields. Who could be doing it, from where?"

"Unknown," answered Spock. "However, I have studied the geology of Playamar, and there are extensive underground caverns. A powerful forcefield generator aimed at the crust could duplicate seismic waves. This would create the effect we are calling aftershocks."

"For what purpose?" asked Raelius.

McCoy snapped his fingers. "To get the colonists off the planet! Spock, didn't you tell me a neighboring race didn't want this colony to be built here?"

Spock nodded. "The Danai. As members of the Federation, they would have access to a powerful forcefield generator."

The captain pounded her fist on the table. "All right, I am pulling you three off the rescue detail to pursue this. But I'm shorthanded. It had better turn up something quickly."

"We need the ship's sensors," said Spock, "to scan the caverns for life signs."

"We've probably already done it." Raelius opened up her communicator. "Captain Raelius to the bridge."

A voice answered, "This is Commander Inzolar."

"Commander, there are deep caverns on the planet. Have we done a scan to see if there are any life signs in those caverns?"

"One moment," said Commander Inzolar. The moment was tense as McCoy gazed at Captain Raelius, wondering if this was a wild-goose chase.

"Captain," said the voice from the bridge. "We have some distorted readings that might be life signs in the bottom level of the Gemming Cavern. No more than six beings. I can send you coordinates."

"Very well," said Raelius. "And send three armed Security officers to the shuttlebay." She turned to McCoy. "I can't arm a bunch of cadets, but I can send a Security team with you. Is that all right?"

"We'll be careful, sir," vowed McCoy.

After reviewing the data from the Gemming Cavern, Captain Raelius decided that there were living beings down there. It was impossible to tell what species they were, or their exact location. There was plenty of space to transport down, because the caverns had huge cathedral-like chambers.

Captain Raelius cleared her throat. "We don't want to cause an uproar about this theory until we're sure. As far as everyone else is concerned, we're sending a rescue party to check out these life signs. Because of conditions, you have an escort."

Raelius glanced at the red-shirted Security detail of two men and one woman. Then she turned back to the cadets. "'You are not to be heroes. Just report what you find. Are we sure it's safe to be that far underground with the aftershocks?"

"It is safer than being on the surface, Captain," answered Spock. "That level of the Gemming Caverns is in bedrock, so there is no danger of liquefaction."

Captain Raelius turned to the security officers. "My team has two missions—to rescue people, and to investigate the aftershocks. Set your phasers to stun, but do what you must to protect them. I want everyone back in one piece, and quickly. We can't spare anybody."

"Yes, sir," snapped Ensign Yermakov, the leader of the Security detail.

Raelius took a deep breath. "If we can stop the aftershocks, it would save a lot of lives. If there are more storms, we may not be able to beam you out of there right away. You may have to spend some time in those caverns."

McCoy gulped. "How long?"

"Until we can beam you out. Maybe you can climb out, but I doubt it. Take emergency rations and water."

"Yes, sir," said McCoy, getting a frightened chill. He had already transported once today, and now he was going to transport through solid rock. All with ion storms that could scramble him for good. What fun.

Ten minutes later, after strapping on extra canteens and rations, McCoy stepped up on the transporter platform. Spock, Lisa, and the three officers in red were already waiting for him. Well, at least there were no jetpacks this time, he thought with relief.

He sure hoped that Spock was right—that it was safe to be underground during an aftershock. Whether they were natural or induced, the quakes were still a nightmare, especially in a dark place with no escape.

"I'll be putting you down in Pharoah's Chamber," said the gray-haired transporter chief.

"Pharoah's Chamber?" asked McCoy.

"That's just the name. There's plenty of room, and it's close to the location of the survivors."

McCoy nodded. "Go ahead."

He screwed his eyes shut as a strange tingling overcame his senses. Was it more intense because they were transporting through rock, or did he just imagine that? The first change he noticed in his surroundings was the cool, dry air. Then he noticed his footing wasn't very steady, and he stumbled off a pile of rocks.

McCoy dropped into a pile of dust that shot into his nostrils and made him sneeze.

"Quiet," cautioned Spock.

McCoy sniffed. "You can't stop a sneeze."

"I can," said the Vulcan.

The medic scowled and tried to accustom his eyes to the darkness. It was an abrupt change from the bright lights of the hospital ship. The others in his party were shining their lights around the vast cavern, and it looked like an old newsreel of an air raid at night.

The beams crisscrossed and revealed huge stalactites hanging from the ceiling and stalagmites forming underneath them. They looked like the monstrous teeth of a dragon, as seen from inside the dragon's mouth.

McCoy played his light across a gray stalactite. He expected to see it glistening and dripping. Instead it looked aged and dry, caked with the dust of millennia.

"Where's the water?" asked Lisa. "Why isn't it dripping?"

"These are dead caves," answered Spock. "Also known as dry caves. The formation of the chambers, stalactites, and stalagmites happened millions of years ago. I estimate that these caves have been dry for eight hundred years."

"Even with all that water on the surface?" asked McCoy.

"Down here," answered Spock, "there is no source of water. However, it is not entirely safe."

The Vulcan shined his light across the cave floor, which was littered with broken stalactites and stalagmites. Some of them were chunks taller than a man.

"The aftershocks have not caused liquefaction here," said Spock "but they have caused many of these formations to crumble."

"It's a tragedy," said Lisa angrily.

Ensign Yermakov snapped his tricorder shut. "I detect life-forms at less than four hundred meters. May I suggest we talk less and proceed with caution."

"Be my guest, sir," said McCoy, motioning the red-shirted trio forward.

In silence, they shuffled through a dark cathedral of gaping teeth and crumbled ruins. McCoy was content to follow the Security detail. He looked around, trying to imagine that an underground sea had once filled this chamber. Now it was dry, dusty, and silent, like an old library.

Pharoah's Chamber must have been the size of a football field, because McCoy was winded by the time the passageway narrowed. After ten meters it became completely blocked, and they couldn't get through. It took frantic searching with tricorders to locate a narrow slit that led to the next chamber.

McCoy hung back and let the others go ahead of him. He couldn't believe they were going to crawl through a crack in the rock. The others soon disappeared into the dark hole, and he was left alone in the cavern. It was completely silent. He could almost swear he could hear the dust falling.

McCoy got down on his hands and knees and scurried into the crack. After walking under cathedral-like ceilings, it seemed strange crawling through a dusty slit. The darkness enveloped him, and McCoy lowered his head and plunged forward.

Without knowing where he was going, he bumped into Lisa's rear end. "Excuse me," he whispered.

"I had to stop," she said. "The ensign sees lights up ahead."

"Lights?" asked McCoy. "Keep going."

He didn't mean to sound so forceful, but his order got the line of people moving again. Like a sluggish snake, they inched their way through the narrow passageway. McCoy just wanted to get off his knees and stand erect again. Finally, the passageway widened, and he staggered forward into a crouch.

He found the others bunched at the entrance to another

vast chamber. The golden glow of a work lamp was clearly visible behind a fallen stalactite. In the bizarre landscape of the cavern, the lamp looked like a peaceful campfire.

Spock gazed at his tricorder. "There are no life signs in the immediate vicinity. They are approximately two hundred meters ahead of us."

Ensign Yermakov nodded and strode toward the light. He didn't draw his phaser, but his hand was on it. In the spacious cavern, the party spread out and moved forward in silence. McCoy was awed by the sight of more giant stalactites suspended from the ceiling.

Cautiously they neared the work light and the fallen stalactite. McCoy breathed a sigh to see that Spock was correct—there was no one around. The lamp illuminated a workbench where somebody had left a complex piece of equipment in midrepair.

"Is that the forcefield generator?" asked Lisa.

Spock studied his tricorder. "No, the forcefield generator is in a smaller cavern adjoining this one. This would appear to be a repair station."

"There's no doubt about it," said McCoy, "somebody is living and working down here."

One of the security officers bent down to inspect the device on the workbench. As soon as he touched it, an alarm began shrieking!

"Oh, no!" muttered McCoy, stumbling away from the howling siren. There was nowhere to hide! He aimed his light down the length of the cavern, expecting to see a horde of armed guards come rushing toward them. Ensign Yermakov stepped forward and drew his phaser.

McCoy pointed his light down the length of the cav-

ern. Finally the beam found one of them! A muscular humanoid crouched in the mouth of the cavern. He was bald except for a strip of hair that started midforehead and went over his skull and down his spine. He had no weapon, and he ducked out of sight.

"All right," said McCoy. "They've seen us, and we've seen them."

Spock nodded. "Retreat would appear to be in order."

McCoy snapped open his communicator. "Gamma team to *Nightingale.*"

"Raelius here. Report."

"We're in the cavern, and there *is* something going on." Suddenly, McCoy felt a dry prickling on the hairs of his neck. His nose dried out, as if a bolt of static electricity had suddenly hit him. That was when he realized what what was happening.

"Beam us up!" he shouted, but it was too late, as the rocks around him began to shudder. An invisible wave knocked McCoy off his feet onto a pile of rocks. He could hear his comrades shouting as they fell all around him.

The world vibrated as the forcefield ripped through the crust of Playamar. Painfully, with rocks poking his back, McCoy rolled over. The only light in the vast chamber was the work lamp, and it bounced around, making crazy shadows on the wall. In one of those shadows, McCoy saw what looked like a giant white shark racing toward him.

Not a shark, his mind screamed, *a stalactite!*

A giant icicle of calcified minerals plummeted toward him.

Chapter
10

McCoy rolled out of the way and kept rolling. He thought the stalactite was going to crush him, until a phaser beam streaked over his head. Half of the stalactite exploded, scattering dust and debris everywhere. The other half fell to the floor of the cave with a horrible crunch.

Panting, McCoy felt his chest to make sure he was still alive. He was cut and bruised, but not crushed. The aftershock suddenly ended, and he looked up to see Ensign Yermakov pointing his phaser at the stalactite.

"Thanks," he croaked.

"No problem," said the Starfleet Security officer. He made an adjustment on the phaser, probably setting it back to stun.

The lamp fell over with a clatter, and it was dark inside the cavern. "Sound off!" shouted McCoy.

"Donald here!" called Lisa.

"Spock here," said the Vulcan's calm voice.

One by one, the three security officers announced that they were still alive. Everyone in the landing party was still accounted for, which was a relief.

"I'll tell them to beam us up." McCoy started to open his communicator.

"That is pointless." Spock stared at his tricorder, which glowed green on his face. "Ion levels are much higher. The *Nightingale* will not be able to transport us for an hour or more."

McCoy shut his communicator. No doubt the Vulcan was right. On the surface of Playamar, the survivors and relief teams were going through the turmoil of another aftershock. Only a handful of people knew that they were artificial quakes.

"Okay, it's up to us," said the medic. "How many of them are there?"

"Six," answered Spock.

With a whistle, a flare shot to the roof of the cavern and exploded. A ball of sparks floated down, lighting up the cavern like a candle in a pumpkin. McCoy could see humanoids stalking the far end of the chamber.

"Down!" he shouted.

He hurled himself back onto the rocks as a disruptor beam went screaming over his head. It blasted off the tip of a stalagmite. The Security officers leapt to their feet and returned fire. Beams streaked wildly around the vast chamber, and McCoy covered his head.

The fighting stopped when the flare's light went out and the cavern was again plunged into darkness. McCoy fumbled for his communicator and opened it up. "Gamma team to *Nightingale.* Come in, Captain Raelius!"

"I'm here, Cadet, what is it?"

"We're under attack!" He hardly needed to explain as another disruptor beam blasted the mineral formation behind him. Chunks of it showered down upon his head.

"Can you identify the hostiles?" asked Raelius calmly.

"Yes. They are hairless except for a strip of hair on their skulls—like a Mohawk."

"Then it is the Danai," said Raelius. "Spock was right."

It became deathly still in the dark cavern, except for some ominous scuffling sounds. "Captain," said McCoy urgently, "we need to beam out of here."

"Sorry. Transporters are down until the ion storms clear."

"Spock was right about that, too," grumbled McCoy.

"Try to reason with the hostiles," said the captain. "If that doesn't work, retreat. As soon as possible, we'll send down reinforcements."

McCoy gulped. "Yes, sir. Gamma team out."

In the darkness, he didn't know how many others had heard the captain's orders. He didn't even know if all of his comrades were still alive. McCoy guessed that it was up to him to try to reason with the saboteurs.

"Listen!" he called out. "We're a Federation rescue team! We know you are Danai. We know what you're doing and where you are. Give yourselves up—don't make it worse!"

The response was a disruptor beam that streaked

across the darkness and scorched a hole in a massive stalagmite. From nowhere, Yermakov leapt to his feet and fired in the direction of the beam. McCoy heard a groan and the sound of a weapon clatter to the floor of the cave.

"Heavy stun," whispered Yermakov with satisfaction. "That stops them. Set phasers for heavy stun."

"Yes, sir," answered each of the other two officers.

McCoy crawled toward the ensign's voice. "What do we do next? I tried reasoning with them."

"You heard the captain—retreat. If they send up an-other flare, the three of you take off for the passageway behind us. We'll cover your retreat."

"What about the three of you?" asked Lisa with concern.

"This is what we are trained to do," answered Yerma-kov. "We'll try to keep them occupied."

McCoy heard a popping sound, and a wavering flare shot up to the roof of the cavern. It exploded in a burst of orange light, and McCoy began to scurry across the rocky floor.

There was action all around him, as the Security offi-cers jumped to their feet and returned fire. Deadly beams crisscrossed the chamber, and Lisa scrambled over a rock and rolled on top of McCoy.

"Sorry!" she gasped. A beam sizzled across their backs and blasted into a stalagmite. It tipped over and crashed to the ground like a petrified tree. As they stared at the amazing sight, Spock crawled past them.

"I suggest you keep moving," said the Vulcan.

Lisa followed him, but McCoy turned around to see two of the Security officers firing at the same target. A Danai spun around and crashed to the floor of the cave. Two down, thought McCoy. *Maybe we're winning!*

Then a disruptor beam caught the female officer in the shoulder. She groaned and dropped to her stomach. McCoy almost started back to help her, but the light from the flare was dying out. A second later, they were plunged back into darkness.

"Come on!" urged Lisa from somewhere in the gloom.

McCoy felt terrible guilt at leaving a wounded officer.

This was against all of his instincts, the Hippocratic oath he planned to take. But his orders were to retreat. He suddenly realized that Starfleet demanded an allegiance beyond a vow to help people.

Another flare streaked to the roof—in the light, he could see the wounded officer. She wasn't that far away. He turned his back on escape and crawled back to help the wounded woman.

"You'll be all right," he told her, but she was already unconscious. As the battle raged around him, McCoy worked swiftly. First he gave her a hypo to stabilize her vital signs, then he cauterized her wound to stop the bleeding.

The light from the flare began to fade, and McCoy looked up and saw Yermakov slumped across a broken stalagmite. He gazed across the eerie battlefield to see three Danai lying unconscious on the ground. But three more of them were advancing on his position.

Then the flare died and the cavern went dark again.

McCoy wanted to stay and help the wounded, but that was the enemy out there. They were shooting to kill! His hands shook as he finished his work and prepared to escape. Crawling on his stomach, he cut a path through the dust and debris.

He had no idea how close he was to the passageway until two strong arms reached out to grab him.

"Quiet," whispered Spock. "This way."

Since McCoy couldn't see anything, he let the Vulcan guide him into the narrow slit in the wall. He hit his head on the rock but didn't cry out in pain. Keeping his head low, he just kept crawling, like a blind mole.

He could hear Spock shuffling along behind him. Only when they were several meters into the passageway did Spock turn on his light so they could see their way. McCoy spotted Lisa just ahead of him.

"What's happening back there?" she asked.

McCoy shook his head. "One of our people got wounded, and I tried to help her. I'm afraid they're all wounded, or worse. There are three Danai left conscious."

"Are they coming after us?"

As if answer to her question, the cavern behind them lit up with another flare. That made all three of the cadets scurry toward the opposite end.

McCoy was relieved when the passageway widened, and he could again stand up. They had escaped the Danai, at least for the moment, but he didn't feel like celebrating. He was bruised and battered, and his knees and elbows were bleeding.

The medic lifted his light to peer into the faces of Lisa and Spock, and they didn't look much better. All three of them were breathing hard. Worse, they were alone and unarmed, and saboteurs were after them.

McCoy leaned against the wall of the cave and wiped the blood from his right elbow. "We're in a real pickle."

"A quaint but accurate assessment," said Spock. He checked his tricorder. "Three of them are gathered at the other end of the passageway. They are probably deciding whether to come after us."

Lisa looked around at the vast Pharoah's Chamber. "How long can we hide from them in here?"

"Unknown," answered Spock. "And we cannot be rescued as long as they can create the ion storms."

"We've got to do something," said McCoy, slamming his fist into his palm. Spock and Lisa looked at him expectantly, waiting for his orders.

McCoy tried to think. He had the crazy idea that they should mount an ambush against their pursuers. But that went against all of his instincts and ideals.

He had come to the academy to *help* people, not to fight them. It all went back to the difference between being a private doctor and a Starfleet doctor. His personal feelings didn't matter when he had a duty to perform.

"We've got wounded officers in there who need help," said McCoy. "At the moment, there are only three Danai, because the others are stunned. But that stun is going to wear off in a few minutes. I say we *ambush* them."

"It's three against three," said Lisa. "We've got no weapons—just our bare hands. I know tae kwon do."

Spock lifted his chin. "I am capable of defending myself."

McCoy picked up a rock. "We'll have the element of surprise." He put his fingers to his lips to tell his comrades to be silent. Then he shouted loudly, "Come on! I see a way out!"

McCoy ran in place, making loud footsteps but not going anywhere. Lisa and Spock did the same, then they pressed themselves against the wall near the passageway. Spock turned off his light and his tricorder, plunging them into darkness.

McCoy held his breath, wondering if their ruse would work. Then he wondered if he would ever see Earth or his family again. Finally he heard scuffling sounds in the narrow passageway, and he could see a dim light bobbing along. McCoy lifted his rock over his head.

In the wavering light, he could see Spock poised like a statue beside the opening. Finally a bald head jutted from the slit, followed by muscular shoulders. Before the Danai could crawl all the way out, Spock did an amazing thing. He reached down and pinched the humanoid on the back of his neck.

The Danai slumped to the ground, unconscious. Spock grabbed him under his shoulders and pulled him out, as Lisa grabbed his weapon. The whole maneuver took only a few seconds and hardly made a sound.

Another unsuspecting Danai emerged from the slit. He rose to his knees before Lisa whirled around with her boot and caught him in the mouth. He slumped to the ground, making a little more noise than the other one.

The third Danai poked his head out of the slit and started to aim his weapon. From above, McCoy dropped the rock on his bald head. He thudded to the ground, joining his comrades in a stupor.

McCoy took out his medical scanner and ran it over each one's bald cranium. "We haven't killed them, but they'll sure have headaches. I want to check on our wounded in the other cavern."

"I'll come with you," said Lisa. "We need to subdue all of the Danai."

"I will attend to these three," said Spock. With rope

from his pack, he trussed up a muscular Danai like a Thanksgiving turkey.

"What was that thing you did to him?" asked McCoy. "All you did was touch his neck."

"Incorrect. I pinched certain nerves at the base of his neck and rendered him unconscious."

"If you say so," answered McCoy. "I never saw such a thing before." He turned on his belt light and headed back into the narrow slit. He could hear Lisa trailing behind him.

When they reached the other cavern, Lisa picked up a fallen phaser. She delivered light stuns to the Danai until Spock arrived to help her tie them up.

For an hour, McCoy tended to the three wounded Security officers. It was touch and go with one of them, but he found himself amazingly calm as he worked. He definitely preferred saving lives, even with its immense responsibility, to commanding others.

Spock and Lisa helped him. When the condition of the wounded officers improved, the two of them went into the adjoining cavern to find the forcefield generator. They returned ten minutes later.

"We disabled it," said Spock. "There will be no more aftershocks on Playamar."

"Good," said McCoy with a sigh.

"They had quite a setup," added Lisa. "It looks as if they've been down here for months."

McCoy glanced at his patients. "Their condition is stabilized, but I really want to get them back to the *Nightingale*. I wonder when we'll be able to leave?"

Suddenly, the entire cavern lit up with dozens of swirling columns of light. As the cadets stared in amazement, thirty red-shirted Security officers materialized all around them. They leveled their phasers, ready for action.

McCoy grinned. "I guess the transporters are running again."

Chapter 11

Without the aftershocks, the rescue effort went swiftly. Survivors were pulled from unsafe buildings, and the injured were transported to hospitals. McCoy, Lisa, and Spock ended up assisting at a field hospital. There was still lots of work to be done rebuilding the planet, but the crisis was over.

The *Nightingale* had to stay in orbit, but the Disaster Relief Service Club was sent home on a transport ship, which was much slower. There was plenty of time for people to congratulate Leonard H. McCoy. Everyone seemed to know that he led the team who stopped the aftershocks.

On their last night on the transport, there was a party for the service club in the mess hall. Captain Raelius recognized everyone's brave and selfless acts of courage. In her twenty years of disaster work, she said, she had never seen a more difficult assignment than Playamar.

Then she turned her attention to McCoy and the Gamma team. "Special recognition must go to the Gamma team. Not only did they discover the cause of the aftershocks, they bravely went underground to capture the saboteurs!"

The mess hall shook with wild, sustained applause from sixty cadets. Lisa smiled and dabbed a tear from her eye. Spock looked calm about all the attention, if somewhat puzzled. McCoy could only shake his head, amazed they were still alive.

"That's the last landing party I'm going on," he whispered to Lisa. "Once I'm a doctor, I'll just sit in my office."

"I bet," said Lisa.

"One more thing," said Captain Raelius. "The Danai claim that the trouble was caused by a separatist group from their planet. But they have agreed to make full reparations to the colonists and aid with the rebuilding."

There was more applause, and everyone was in a great mood of camaraderie. McCoy figured that if he would ever have a chance to ask Lisa for a date, this would be it.

Captain Raelius smiled and lifted her glass of sparkling apple cider. "It doesn't seem possible that only a week ago, we were all lifting a glass to welcome our new members. There are no new members anymore. You are all battle-scarred veterans. I salute you, the best service club in Starfleet Academy!"

She drained her glass, and so did everyone else. The applause was wild. It must have rocked the ship.

The captain remembered something. "Oh, yes, Happy

New Year! Tonight is New Year's Eve, and we'll be back in San Francisco half an hour before midnight."

That was the clincher, thought McCoy. Now he had to try to ask Lisa out. He turned to her as she was starting to get up from the table.

"Lisa," he said, "what are you doing for New Year's Eve?"

She gave him a sympathetic smile and sat back down. "I told you, I have a boyfriend. I already called him, and he's meeting me."

"That's right," said McCoy, trying to sound brave. "Who is this lucky guy?"

"You don't know him. He's just a first-year cadet."

He frowned at her. "What his name?"

"Jim Kirk."

McCoy slapped his forehead and groaned. "Not James T. Kirk?"

"Do you know him?"

"I wouldn't be here except for him."

"Yeah, he's a great guy, isn't he?" Cheerfully, Lisa got up and walked away.

McCoy turned around and saw Spock looking at him. "What do you want?"

The Vulcan straightened in his seat. "I want nothing. I do feel the effects of lack of sleep. Several hours of sleep would be most refreshing."

"So you're going to sleep on New Year's Eve," said McCoy, shaking his head. "Are you really half human?"

"Biologically," answered Spock. "In every other sense, I am Vulcan."

"Stick with Vulcans. You wouldn't want to serve with humans."

"Perhaps I would," answered Spock. He looked around at the boisterous celebration. "They can be fascinating."

Humans could also be lonely, thought McCoy, as he waited in line to beam down to Starfleet Academy. Most of the cadets had formed bonds with their teams, and they hung out in the same threesomes. McCoy stood by himself at the end of the line. Lisa was far ahead of him, anxious to get down to her boyfriend, that dunderhead, Kirk.

Spock stood nearby, but McCoy doubted whether he could talk the Vulcan out of his stimulating plans to sleep. He supposed he could tag along with a group of cadets, but he didn't know if he had the energy to be sociable. Maybe Spock was right—sleep wasn't such a bad idea.

When it was his turn to beam down, McCoy screwed his eyes shut. He didn't care how many times he transported, it would never feel natural or healthy. He stepped off the transporter platform and was checked in by an ensign. Transporter duty on New Year's Eve, thought McCoy. That's what Starfleet is all about.

He stepped out of the building and felt the nippy air, full of salt and sea smells. It reminded McCoy of Sunshine Hamlet, and he shivered and pulled up the collar of his new jacket. It was not the same jacket as before, as the first one had gotten destroyed.

"Handsome jacket you got there," said a voice.

McCoy whirled around and saw his gray-haired father step out of the shadows. He held out his arms. "Welcome home, Son."

"Dad!" McCoy rushed to give his dad a hug, then he shook his hand like a long-lost friend. "Dad, what are you doing here?"

"When I got your message and I heard about Playamar, I started following the story. They said you were coming back today, so I took a shuttle. If you can't come to see me, there's no reason why I can't come to you. Besides, you can't be alone on New Year's Eve."

"No, Dad, you can't." McCoy gripped his father's arm, making sure he was real flesh and blood.

"How about some late dinner? Then you can tell me all about your adventures. By gosh, it's good to see you, Leonard."

"You, too, Dad," said McCoy with a grin. "First of all, do you have any idea how strong Vulcans are?"

"Strong, huh?"

"Let me tell you . . ." The McCoys walked down the sidewalk as the mists of San Francisco floated across the campus green.

About the Author

JOHN VORNHOLT was born in Marion, Ohio, and knew he wanted to write science fiction when he discovered Doc Savage novels and the words of Edgar Rice Burroughs. But somehow he wrote nonfiction and television scripts for many years, including animated series such as *Dennis the Menace, Ghostbusters,* and *Super Mario Brothers.* He was also an actor and playwright, with several published plays to his credit.

John didn't get back to his first love—writing SF—until 1989 with the publication of his first Star Trek Next Generation novel, *Masks.* He wrote two more, *Contamination* and *War Drums;* a classic Trek novel, *Sanctuary;* and a Deep Space Nine novel, *Antimatter.* For young readers, he's also written *Starfleet Academy #4: Capture the Flag.* All of these titles are available from Pocket Books.

John is also the author of several nonfiction books for kids and the novel *How to Sneak into the Girls' Locker Room.*

John lives in Tucson, Arizona, with his wife, Nancy, his children, Sarah and Eric, and his dog, Bessie.

About the Illustrator

TODD CAMERON HAMILTON is a self-taught artist who currently lives in Kalamazoo, Michigan. He has been a professional illustrator for the past ten years, specializing in fantasy, science fiction, and horror. Todd is the current president of the Association of Science Fiction and Fantasy Artists. His original works grace many private and corporate collections. He has coauthored two novels and several short stories. When he is not drawing, painting, or writing, his interests include metalsmithing, puppetry, and teaching.